How to Be a Man

Stories

Tamara Linse

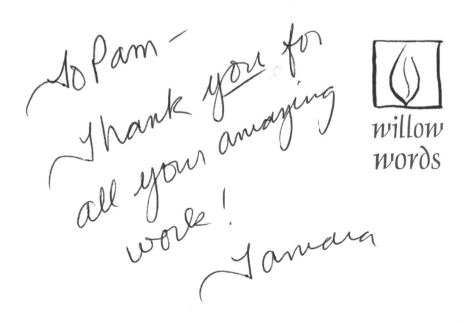

To Pam —
Thank you for
all your amazing
work!
Tamara

willow
words

This collection in a slightly different form was a semifinalist for the
Black Lawrence Press Hudson Prize

These stories were originally published in the following publications:

"A Dangerous Shine" in Word Riot
"Control Erosion" in SNReview
"Dammed" in the South Dakota Review
"How to Be a Man" in New West
"In the Headlights" in roger
"Men Are Like Plants" in Slow Trains
"Oranges" in Ramble Underground
"Revelations" in Fried Chicken and Coffee
"The Body Animal" in Talking River
"Wanting" in the Georgetown Review

These stories were finalists for following awards:

"Hard Men" for the Reynolds Price Short Fiction Award
"In the Headlights" for the Glimmer Train Short-Story Award for New
    Writers
"Wanting" for the Georgetown Review short story contest

Cover photo courtesy Doreen Salcher, www.deefoto.de

<u>Print</u>   <u>Epub</u>
ISBN: 0991386701   ISBN: 099138671X
ISBN-13: 978-0-9913867-0-3   ISBN-13: 978-0-9913867-1-0

Edition 1.1

To Steve, the foundation under my feet
and the grit I rub against

Contents

"If you're white, and you're not rich or poor but somewhere in the middle, it's hard to have worse luck than to be born a girl on a ranch."

Maile Meloy
"Ranch Girl"
The New Yorker

How to Be a Man

How to Be a Man

NEVER ACKNOWLEDGE THE FACT THAT YOU'RE A GIRL, and take pride when your guy friends say, "You're one of the guys." Tell yourself, "I am one of the guys," even though, in the back of your mind, a little voice says, "But you've got girl parts."

You are born on a ranch in central Colorado or southern Wyoming or northern Montana and grow up surrounded by cowboys. Or maybe not a ranch, maybe a farm, and you have five older brothers. Your first memory is of sitting on the back of Big Cheese, an old sorrel gelding with a sway back and— you find out later when you regularly ride bareback—a backbone like a ridge line. Later, you won't know if this first memory is real or comes from one of the only photos of you as a baby. You study that photo a lot. It must be spring or late fall because you're wearing a quilted yellow jacket with a blue-lined hood and your brother's hands reach from the side of the frame and support you in the saddle. You look half asleep with your head tilted to the side against your shoulder, a little sack of potatoes.

Your dad is a kind man, a hard worker, who gives you respect when no one else will. When you're four, if he asks,

"Birdie, do you think the price of hogs is going up?" ponder this a while. Take into account how Rosie has just farrowed seven piglets and how you're bottle-raising the runt and how you've heard your brothers complaining about pig shit on the boots they wear to town. Think about how much Jewel—that's what you've decided to name the pig—means to you and say, "Yes, Daddy, pigs are worth a lot." He'll nod his head, but he won't smile like other people when they think what you say was cute or precocious.

Your mother is a mouse of a woman who takes long walks in the gray sagebrushed hills beyond the fields or lays in the cool back bedroom reading the Bible. When your brothers ask "Where's Mom?" you won't know. You don't think it odd when at five you learn how to boil water in the big speckled enamelware pot and to shake in three boxes of macaroni, to watch as it turn from off-yellow plasticity to soft white noodles, to hold both handles with a towel and carefully pour it into the colander in the sink while avoiding the steam, to measure the butter and the milk—one of your brothers shows you how much—and then to mix in the powdered cheese. You learn to dig a dollop of bacon grease from the Kerr jar in the fridge into the hot cast iron skillet, wait for it to melt, and then lay in half-frozen steaks, the wonderful smell of the fat and the popping of ice crystals filling the kitchen. When your brothers come in from doing their chores, they talk and laugh instead of opening the cupboards and slamming them shut. And your dad doesn't clench his jaw while washing his hands with Dawn dishwashing liquid at the kitchen sink and then toss big hunks of Wonder Bread into bowls filled with milk.

When you wear hand-me-downs from your brothers, be proud. Covet the red plaid shirt of your next older brother, and when you get it—a hot late summer afternoon when he tosses three shirts on your bed—wear it until the holes in the elbows decapitated the cuffs. If you go to town with your dad for parts, be proud of your shitty boots and muddy jeans and torn-up shirts. It shows that you know an honest day's work. Work is more important than fancy things, and you are not one of those ninnies who wear girlie dresses and couldn't change a tire if their lives depended on it.

Be prepared: when you go to school, you won't know quite where you fit. All the other kids will seem to know something that you don't, something they whisper to each other behind their hands. They won't ever whisper it to you. But they won't make fun of you either because—you'll get this right away and take pride in it—you are tough and also you have five older brothers and the Gunderson family sticks together. Be proud of the fact that, in seventh grade social studies, you sit elbows-on-the-table next to a boy about your size, and he says with a note of admiration, "Look at them guns. You got arms bigger than me." It's winter, and you've been throwing hay bales every morning to feed the livestock.

Your friends will be boys. You understand boys. When you say something, they take it at face value. If they don't understand, hit them, and they'll understand that. For a couple of months—until your dad finds out about it—your second oldest brother will give you a dime every time you get into a fist fight. The look on your brother's face as he hands you those dimes will make your insides puff to bursting. Use the dimes to buy lemons at the corner grocery during lunch time.

3

Slice them up with your buck knife and hand them out to see which of the boys can bite into it without making a face.

Leave the girls alone, and they will leave you alone. When you have to be together, like in gym class, they'll ignore you, which will be fine with you. Always take the locker by the door so you can jet in and out as fast as you can. You'll be mortified that they'll see your body, how gross and deformed it is. Be proud of the muscles, but the buds of breast and the peaking pubic hair will be beyond embarrassing. Still, you'll be fascinated with their bodies, not in a sexual way, but in that they seem to be so comfortable with them, even—to your disgust—proud. They'll compare boobs in the mirror, holding their arms up against their ribs so that their breasts push forward. One girl, Bobbie Joe Blanchard, won't stand at the mirror though because she'll get breasts early, big round ones. She'll quickly go from a slip of a girl who never says anything to the most popular because the boys pay attention, and the attention of the boys is worth much more than any giggling camaraderie of the girls. You'll agree with this, but you'll also be mystified as to the boys' motivations. Ask your best friend Jimmy Mockler, "What's up with that?" He'll just shrug and smile, sheepishly but with pride too.

In middle school, don't be surprised if the guys who used to be your friends forget about you. They'll still be nice, but they'll spend their time playing rough games of basketball and daring each other to talk to this girl or that. You won't be good at basketball—you're tough, but you don't have the height or the competitiveness. Plus, they don't really want you to play—you can tell. Think about this a lot, how to regain their respect. Go so far as to ask the coach about trying out for football. He'll look at you like you're a two-headed calf and say, "Darlin', girls don't play football." You'll want to scream, "I'm not a girl!" but you won't. Instead, never tell anyone, especially the boys, and hope to God that the coach never mentions it in gym class, which he teaches. He won't. He'll agree with you that it's embarrassing.

One day at lunch time, Jimmy Mockler will tell a story to the other guys about Bobbie Joe Blanchard and how he's asked her to meet him under the bleachers in the gym during fifth period study hall. There is no gym during fifth period. He and Bobbie Joe are going to get passes to go to the bathroom and sneak in when no one's looking. "I bet she lets me kiss her!" he says and laughs and the other boys laugh. Then he says, "Maybe she'll even give me a hand job." He'll glance at you and this look of horror will come over his face. They'll all look at you. Right then you'll know you've lost them. At home that night, cry in your room without making a sound in case your brothers walk by.

Realize at this point that you have two choices: either you have to win back the boys or you have to throw in with the girls. But you don't understand the girls at all. You wouldn't know the first thing about it. How do you talk to girls, anyway? Don't lose heart. Maybe there is a way to make it through to the boys. If pretty girls are what gets their attention, maybe you'll have to learn to look like a girl, even if you aren't really one. You can learn. Didn't you teach yourself how to make peach pies from scratch? How to braid horsehair into hat bands? How to pick the lock on the second oldest brother's bottom drawer, only to be disgusted with the magazines you found there? You can do this.

5

Imagine the looks on the boys' faces. The admiration filling their eyes. Respect, even. And the jealousy in the girls' eyes. Jimmy will walk up to you and put his arm around you and say, "Where you been?" There'll be no more awkward silences, no more conversations that switch when you walk up. It'll be the same as before, once they notice you. All you have to do is get their attention.

Raid your mom's closet for a dress. Smuggle it into your room. It's the one you've seen her wear to church—knee-length, sky blue with a white scalloped collar. You are her height now, and it'll fit you. To your surprise, you'll even fill it out in the bust. Surreptitiously steal a copy of a girls' magazine from the library and study it—the way the girls' hair is curled, the way their lips shine, how clean their hands are. Decide to try it the following Monday. Sunday night, take a long bath and try to soak off all the dirt and scrub the elephant hide off your feet. The leg bruises from working in the barn won't come off, but sacrifice your toothbrush to scrub your fingernails. Tie up your wet hair in rags like you've seen your mother do on Saturday nights before Sunday church services. The next morning, get ready in your room so no one will see you. Climb into the dress. You will feel naked and drafty around the legs. This is normal. Brush out your hair. Instead of nice wavy curls, it will stuck out all over the place. Wet it down just a little, which will help, but it will still look like an alfalfa windrow. You don't have any lip gloss, so use bag balm, the sticky yellow substance you put on cow teats when they chap. This won't really be new because when your lips crack from sun or wind burn, that's what you use. It will feel different though.

Look at yourself in the mirror. You won't recognize yourself. It will be a weird double consciousness—this person in the mirror is you, you'll know it, but you'll have to glance down anyway just to match the image in the mirror with the one attached to your body. Beware. It will creep you out. It looks like a girl in the mirror, but it can't be because you aren't one of them.

Whatever happens, keep telling yourself: it'll be worth it if it works.

Don't go downstairs until just before your brothers are ready to drive to school. When you come down, your brothers will stop talking. The brother just older than you will laugh, but then your dad will whistle and say, "My, don't you look pretty today." This will make you feel a little better and stop the boys' wolf whistles, though they'll keep glancing sideways at you in the car. If the brother just older than you whispers, "Look who's a ger-rel," the oldest one will tap him upside the head to shut him up.

Make your oldest brother drop you off two blocks from school and hide behind a tree until you're sure school has started. You won't want anyone to see you ahead of time. In fact, you'll be having second thoughts about the whole project. Be brave. You'll think of Jimmy Mockler and the embarrassed way he looks at you, maybe even avoids you when you come down the hall, and that'll help. Creep in a side door, scoot to your locker, get your books, and go to homeroom. If you feel like you might let loose in your pants as you peek into the classroom through the wire-latticed window, wait—this will pass. Mrs. Garcia will probably have everyone working in groups, and desks will be pushed together in four messy circles. The guys in the back will be in one group, including Jimmy. Rest your hand on the door knob for a long time, take a deep breath, and then push through the door.

The noise of everyone talking at once will hit you as the door opens. That and the smell of the fish tank and Mrs. Garcia's sickeningly sweet perfume. Stutter-breathe and make a beeline toward the boy's circle. Talking will begin to peter out as you enter the room, and you'll make it halfway along the wall toward the back before there's dead silence. Everyone will be looking at you, but keep your eyes on the boys' circle. The looks on the boys' faces will be wonderful. All their eyes fastened on you, looking admiringly, small smiles in the corners of their mouths. They will be looking at you, noticing you. Jimmy, particularly, will have a wide-eyed slack-jawed grin on his face.

Celebrate. You've done it. You've regained their attention. You are once more an honorary boy, respected and included.

But then it'll be like a slow-motion horror movie. From behind you, Mrs. Garcia will say, "Why, Birdie Gunderson, I almost didn't recognize you." Watch these words register on the boys' faces. Some of them will give a little shrug and turn back toward the others, but it's Jimmy's reaction that will bruise you to the core. You'll see the time delay of the words entering his ears and then his brain and then the look on his face fix as his brain processes the words and then his eyes widen as he finally understands. Then, it'll be as if someone grabs the center of his face and twists. The look will be so awful your body will wander to a stop, and you'll stand, unbelieving, still caught in the adrenalin of the moment before. You're going to cry, so flip around and push back out through the door and run down the hall and out the big double doors by the principal's office. Run until you can't breathe and then walk, taking in big hiccupping breaths of air, all the way to the high school. Make your oldest brother take you home.

Accept your fate. You'll never regain that special place with the boys, and you become a second-hand friend. Every once in a while your brothers will say, "Remember the time Birdie tried to be a girl?" and they'll laugh. Laugh with them. You know how ridiculous it was.

High school will be a long lonely blur, but take it like a man. Never go on a date, never kiss a boy. Instead, watch football and memorize the stats and, if anyone tries to strike up a conversation, bring up the Dallas Cowboys. Take your one stab at getting outside your life—after high school, go to community college for a semester, but when your mom dies of some unnamable female ailment, your dad will need you on the farm. You'll tell yourself that you can always go back and get that degree, but you won't. Fill your days with the routine of agriculture. The animals won't care if you're a boy or a girl— they just need to be fed and watered. Same with your dad and brothers. Don't think about being a man. Or being a woman. You are an efficient cog in the machinery of the farm.

"Sis, you're the best," they'll all say. "Birdie is as faithful as a hound dog."

You are, you know? You're a good cook, you know a lot about football, and you work hard. It doesn't matter that you don't have any friends, men or women. It doesn't matter that you don't get out much and you'll never be kissed, much less married. When you have needs, take care of them yourself. Don't think about becoming a skinny whiskery-chinned old batty with too many dogs. You're happy. Or at least you're not sad. You're comfortable. You have a full life taking care of your dad and your brothers. You do. You really do.

Or, maybe this isn't the way it goes.

Maybe, when you're in your early thirties, your fourth oldest brother will bring home an old college buddy for two weeks one summer. Conrad Patel. You'll resent the hell out of it, this change in routine. This guy will make you uncomfortable. At first you'll think he's gay because he's thin and has a loose-limbed way of walking. This will make you wonder about your brother. Then you'll understand by the way they talk about women that they're just comfortable with each other. They understand each other. It'll remind you of how it used to be with you and Jimmy Mockler—you'll be sad at first and then angry. Go out of your way to avoid this Conrad Patel. You might even do little things to make yourself feel better, like flushing the downstairs toilet when he's in the upstairs shower. Every time you get the chance.

A lot of your energy during the summer goes into growing the garden, and after your dad and the boys leave for the fields, spend your mornings watering and weeding. In the evening after the supper dishes are done, walk through the garden and inspect things—pollinate the tomatoes, check for potato bugs, and shut the hothouse boxes. You will love this time of cool breeze and setting sun. But it will annoy the hell out of you when Conrad Patel breaks away from the card game or the sitcom TV to follow you out the back door and down the porch steps. He won't seem to understand the very strong hints you drop. Start sneaking out the front door, but don't be surprised if you find him already there in the garden.

"But you don't grow coriander?" Conrad Patel will say. "You don't grow fennel? Not even tarragon?" He will say this with wonder, as if these things are essential to life.

Say, "If you don't like what I cook, don't eat it," and turn your back.

If he says, "Oh no—your cooking is a marvel. So very different from my mother's," you won't be sure how to take this, just like you're never quite sure how to take anything he says. Say, "You're comparing me to your mother?" It will irritate you. Really irritate you. You'll wish you were ten again so you could sock him.

"Yes, of course," he'll say, once again as if this were a given.

Realize that he doesn't understand you any more than you understand him. You won't know what to say so don't say anything and hope that's the end of it.

But it won't be. He'll say, "You would drive across this country to eat her mashed potatoes. The key is browning the mustard seeds, with just enough chilies to make your lips burn. This makes me want to drop everything and go for a visit." His voice will be both intense and wistful.

As you finish up in the garden, he'll talk about cooking but then about his family. He'll tell you about his mother and his aunts and grandmother. Also about his brothers and his dad, who has passed away. It's not what he says so much as how he says it. Women to him are a mystery, much like they are to you, but not in a contemptuous way. He talks about them with such respect and such admiration, like they are men and men are women. To him, women are the source of all goodness and men are the source of all evil. Women are the ones who get things done, the practical ones, and men spend their time being frivolous with money.

It will all be so foreign to you that when he stops talking it'll be as if you walked out of a movie theater. Remind yourself of where you are. And who you are. Your body and your approach to the world will have traveled to another place where what you were supposed to be doesn't seem so far from what you are. You'll want to reject it whole cloth, but there's a part of you that will want to break into tears.

Shut the last hothouse lid and turn to leave.

Conrad Patel will say, "I have said something wrong." He will step in front of you. "What I meant was that your potatoes are the same. Not the same—they don't contain mustard seeds. But the same in that they are wonderful. And your beef stew is wonderful. You are a wonderful woman."

Are you? Do those words go together?

It's dark enough that you won't be able to see his face, but if he steps closer to you, don't step away. He'll stand in front of you and you'll feel the heat of his body through the cool of the evening. You'll like this feeling. You might wonder what's coming, if he's leaning toward you ever so slightly—it will be hard to tell in the fading light. Don't let this frighten you. Don't run away. Face your fears. Be a man.

Men Are Like Plants

IF A GERANIUM WERE A MAN, it'd be a pimp. No kidding. All those showy flowers, sort of like gold chains and purple polyester, don't you think? And those leaves, all romantic ruffle, like the artist formerly known as Prince would wear. And they're persistent. Prolific. Hardy. The whole New York police force couldn't stop 'em. Heck, a nuclear war couldn't stop 'em. The bomb would hit, they'd wilt a little, and as soon as the sun stimulated them—Bam!— another bloom would poke its head up. And the smell—like bad aftershave mixed with pepperoni, persistent and annoying.

Now, your philodendron on the other hand—he's a guy I could get to now. A little bit of pizzazz—those broad split and elegantly arched leaves, so simple and grand, sort of like tuxedo tails, sturdy yet supple. Doesn't move too fast, doesn't rush things, makes his way from the pot to the wall, growing out faithfully and steadily.

Hmmm. Maybe a little too steadily.

Your cacti, now, they're the *nice guys*. You know what I mean. The guys that you just want to be friends with, the ones you think of as brothers. The spines, you ask? Well, of course—you'd get a little prickly too if you were always the last choice, the one asked to the Sadie Hawkins dance only

13

after the girl's best friend's ugly kid brother was already taken. They don't look so sexy, and they're shaped kind of funny, but they're the best guys to have around when you need your car worked on or someone to go to the movies with. Heck, they're probably the best type to marry, too, if you can get past the spines and bulges. I have lots of cacti in my apartment. Like I said, they're great company.

On a first date, I have a question I ask. It's a great litmus test, never fails. I ask, "If you were a plant, what kind would you be?" Sometimes they give me a weird look. I end the date early. Sometimes they laugh outright. If it's a good-natured laugh, that's ok, but if it's one of those you-must-be-one-of-those-hippy-dippy-crystal-beads-and-love-chicks kind of laughs, I split. Some of them take me seriously. These I let kiss me. Heck, if they give a good answer, I screw their brains out. I get a lot of trees—oak trees, pine trees, redwood trees. They have their uses, which don't usually extend more than six inches from their bodies.

"Grass," one guy said. Wow! I thought. Grass. Why would he be grass?

This guy was good looking, short, with dark spiky hair. He was a little soft but lanky. He slouched a lot. We went out for breakfast after the bars closed.

"Yeah," he said. "Grass. Not weed, not that kind of grass, though that'd be fun. Real on-the-lawn grass."

"Grass," I said. "You're the first person who's ever said grass." This could be a bad thing. Maybe he wanted to take over the world. All the grass I know is in stiff competition with the trees to cover as much space as possible. I have these huge flower gardens that I take care of for some rich friends of

14

mine—the most beautiful bougainvillea and nasturtiums, a whole hill of portulaca. Anyway, the grass scales walls or climbs under it or through it, if there's no other way, to lay siege to the flower beds. You can see the flowers beat a hasty retreat, their leaves and stems pumping. The lily-livered bastards run away, and the grass marches on.

"Nah. Don't look at me like that," Spiky-Hair said. "Grass is commonplace, the everyday, like words. Everyone knows grass, everyone uses grass. It surrounds us. We are immersed in its pollen, its sex. We roll in it. It gives us oxygen … or is it carbon dioxide? Whatever. It's my metaphor." He nodded importantly.

"Your metaphor?" I prompted, intrigued.

"Yeah. I hadn't thought about it till just now," he said, "but grass isn't just common. It can be beautiful, like the prairies in the flames of the setting sun, the wind fanning it."

I love this image. This guy had me right here.

"Grass can be exquisite," he continued. "Elegant. Ever seen pampas grass? It can also be utilitarian. Bamboo is a grass, I think. The Japanese use bamboo for everything."

He sipped his coffee and smiled. I smiled back. We called for the check.

However, as it turns out, grass is not particular about who uses it, how many at one time, where, all that. Grass isn't good in a monogamous relationship.

ANOTHER GUY SAYS HE WOULD BE A TOMATO PLANT. We are sitting on some deck chairs in his back yard drinking mai tais.

"A tomato plant?" I ask.

15

"I'd be a tomato plant," he says with finality. He's a little bald, and his body is round and strong. Not in a bad way, though. He wears a polo shirt and dockers.

"Why would you be a tomato plant?" I prompt.

"Because I love them," he continues, sipping his mai tai. "Their smell takes me back to my grandma's garden. Did you ever sneak into your grandmother's garden while the tomatoes were green just so you could sniff the plants? I've driven out of my way just so I could rub the leaves." His eyes are far away. Then he looks at me. "I'd definitely be a tomato. What would you be?"

I am floored, caught flat-footed. You seem shocked—don't be. No guy has ever asked me before. If you discount the ones who laugh and the trees, too busy being independent and virile or trying to pollinate, you have only a couple of guys, some of which are married and thinking only of their stamens. Now we're down to just one or two.

So I am shocked.

"What kind of plant would I be?" I stutter. Now that was a personal question. I'm not sure that I'm ready to share that with him.

Hedging, I say, "Tomatoes are a little finicky. They need lots of attention and warmth."

He doesn't seem to notice the obvious dodge. "Yes, yes," he nods. "I certainly know what I want. I have goals. But that's a good thing, don't you think?"

"Hmmm," I say. "Yeah."

"And I do seek the warmth and light of those I care about. Just as I like to think I shine, I give that warmth back." He grins. "I've got a very attractive odor, too," he says and breaks into a giggle. Yep. It's a giggle, not a chuckle or a laugh, but it sounds good on him.

"What about the whole fruit thing?" I ask.

"Oh, yeah. That's right. Tomatoes are a fruit," he says. "That doesn't sound too good, does it?" His eyes twinkle. "So if I were a sauce, would I pour over the robust manicotti or the lovely angel hair? What do you think?" he says.

"I was hoping you'd be more inclined toward the angel hair, or even the slightly less lovely but much more fulfilling spaghetti," I say.

"You're right. I'm more of a spaghetti man." He cocks an eyebrow. "Though angel hair is not without its charms." He sees my expression and then quickly adds, "But so much preparation. And it doesn't keep well. Spaghetti—now that'll keep for weeks, heck, maybe even months." He laughs.

I laugh.

"Seriously," he continues, "though men can't *bear fruit*, I like to think that I am able to give back, to provide, to …"—he pauses, as if he were looking for just the right word—"to work with others to bring to life something new. Yes, that's it." He nods.

"I don't know many men who would …" It's my turn to hesitate. I'm so impressed at this point that I'm afraid that whatever I say will spoil it. I continue, "Not many men would lay claim to a maternal side."

"Well, I'm not many men, am I?" he replies. "Now quit dodging the question. I've answered fair and square. Your turn. What kind of plant would you be? You've obviously thought about it."

17

YES I HAD.

When I was a child, I wanted to be a flower. Every girl wants to be a flower—specifically a rose. I fervently, feverishly, ardently wanted to be a rose, one of those delicate varieties, Mutabilis or Queen Elizabeth, preferably red. I'd read *Cinderella* and *Snow White* and *The Princess and the Pea*. I wanted to bloom gloriously and to die romantically, maybe in a garret. But then I realized the drawbacks of dying in a garret. Still, though, I wanted to be a flower. I pondered the beautiful elegant columbine, with all its colors, or better yet the delicate white variety with lace and ruffles. Then I realized that I might as well be the rose because the columbine is even more delicate. I'd die in the gutter instead of the garret, and I wouldn't have thorns to protect me.

Questing further, I was still thinking flowers. Then I saw Audrey Hepburn in *Breakfast at Tiffany's* and I was calla lily all the way. Such elegance, such charm. I lost ten pounds and tried on a British accent. I think being a calla lily was good for me. It matured me, gave me poise. I remained a calla lily for a long time, but one day when I was fourteen I was asked to lunch by my best friend Minta. We made it a point to go to the fashionable Café du Paree, all potted palms and fig trees, even though we were only freshman. All the in-crowd seniors hung out there, not the jock in-crowd but the kids with money. I didn't have a lot of money, so Minta treated me. My cousin Jessica started working there. At one time, she was my idol. She had this slender dark-eyed grace that reminded me of a cross between Marlene Dietrich and Twiggy. But she stuttered her *M*s when she was nervous, so she dropped out of my top ten most beautiful people of all time. I still adored her, though.

I will never forget it. She came out to wait on two couples, teenagers, some of the wealthiest kids in town. Beautiful graceful people, calla lilies all the way. They must have said something to her because I could tell she was stuttering. Her eyes were closing spasmodically and her top lip was pressed against the bottom in a desperate attempt to get out an *M*, maybe trying to say *may*, as in "may I get you something." She couldn't do it. She flushed to the roots of her hair. The kids weren't helping her either. They just sat there and snickered. She must have switched her working—"Shall I get you something?" maybe—because soon the couples gave their orders and ignored her. A small incident, I know, but I thought, calla lilies. They're beautiful, yes, but their grace only lasts as long as you water them carefully, worship them, give in to their every whim, their every need. Calla lilies aren't as beautiful and graceful on the inside as they are on the outside.

And then I didn't want to be a calla lily anymore. I had wanted to, and I'd been—or thought I'd been—at least for a while, and it made my skin crawl, the cruelty of it, the way they made Jess blush and stammer. I was no better than them, I realized. I might have even done the same, had it not been Jess. I wasn't a calla lily. I didn't want to be a calla lily. In fact, I was much more of a weed, a kochia or a knapweed, my outsides matching my insides. The world wasn't a garden where carefully tended plants thrived. Rather, it was a back lot where plants strove against one another for survival, where the really beautiful could not live.

THIS MAN, MY TOMATO PLANT, IS LOOKING AT ME EXPECTANTLY.

19

Would he know the gravity of my choice?

I look over at the lilacs, all fluffy purpleness, the miniature crab with delicate sprays of pink, the tulips shouting red, the small flowers—pansies and petunias and cosmos. This back yard is a place where flowers could grow. Looking at the yard and back to him, I realize that these are his flowers, and this is his back yard. He is the one who carefully tends these buds. I look again at the yard, this time with new eyes. It is well tended but not over-tended. You know the yards that nary a dandelion dare rear its head? Every hedge is carefully clipped—and there are always hedges, and straight-line walls, and paths in perfect squares, usually of impermeable brick or cement. The yards where grass is carefully kept at the prescribed 1.75 inches, where everything grows wonderfully but only in its carefully designated area. No. That is not this man. This man—his name is Michael—carefully tends his plants. They glow with riotous good health. They thrive. They also fall over one another in a joyful climb to the sun. Dandelions dot his yard, but so does scarlet globemallow and plantain. His grass is mowed, but in the same way you might prune a rose bush or dead-head flowers. He allows them out of his control, but he doesn't let them run wild. It is as if he were holding a beautiful soap bubble, such a delicate touch. When I realize this, I flush to my toes. This is the man, the man who would understand me, the man I have been waiting for. At that thought, my answer takes on gigantic proportions. Will he understand?

I rattle the ice cubes in my glass. "Looks like my drink's empty. May I have another? *Please*?" I do my best to bat my eyelashes.

He considers. "You're still stalling," he says, his brow wrinkling. "You started it. All right, I'll get you another drink, but when I get back, I expect an answer. Kidding aside." He unfurls and takes my drink.

Would he understand, this obvious lover of plants? Well, I can't lie, can I? I could tell him what he wants to hear. I could tell him that I'm a rose. That was what he wants to hear, isn't it? But then I can't do that to him. As much as I want to—no, need to. I will admit that. I need his approval. If I don't tell him the truth, it would be a lie. What would be a lie? This, all of this. What we have, or will have, if there is going to be an *us*.

He comes back and bows, ceremoniously placing the glass on my arm rest.

"Now," he says, "is the time for all good women to fess up. What plant would you be?" He says this a little too loudly and a little too forcefully. He sits down.

"I would be a ..." I hesitate. I was going to do it, to say *rose*, swear to God. He is too important. This is too important. But then I say, "No. I can't lie. I wouldn't be that." I say this sort of to the back yard and to all these beautiful flowers. I take a deep breath. "I couldn't be a plant," I say.

His eyebrows shoot up. He looks a little angry, as if I'd been making fun of him. His open gaze slams shut. "You wouldn't be ...?" he ventures.

"No, not wouldn't, *couldn't*," I say, mentally berating myself. You should have said *rose*, you idiot. Same-old, same-old. Now this guy thinks I'm fruitier than an apple tree. I continue, "No, I couldn't. I am too ..."—what could I say?—"too impure, too human."

His eyes soften.

21

"What I mean is, I am not worthy to be a plant. They only ask for a little water, a little sun, and a little space. I could never be that humble, that uncomplicated, that pure. It's …" I hesitate again, "it's sort of like zen. I could never be able to elevate myself that much. Plants accept—I am judgmental." On this last word, I fasten my eyes on my drink, not daring to face him. He'll think I'm so stupid.

The silence is heavy. It stretches longer and longer and gets heavier and heavier. I am at the point of jumping out of my chair and leaving when he says, "Hmmm." Just that. I glance over at him. He is looking at a large dandelion blossom that he is twiddling in his fingers. Now I've done it. I've really done it. I start to get up.

"No. Wait," he says. "I don't know what to say."

I hesitate a moment, and then I do get up.

"No, wait!" he says again. "It's just that …" He hesitates. "I'm still absorbing it. Your answer, I mean."

I'm skeptical, and he can tell. I stand very still.

"Your words make me look … well, silly," he finally says. Then he turns his full attention to me, his lips pulled kind of back, not a smile exactly, puzzled, as if he'd stumbled into a rainforest and found a new species, or the possibility of a new species—*or* he's found that the Jones moved in next door and brought out their herbicide.

I still say nothing.

"Tell you what," he says, carefully placing the dandelion in his mai tai, "you don't leave right now, and I won't regret what just happened for the rest of my life."

Oh my God, he still likes me! He's tasted my pith and found it sweet!

A Dangerous Shine

WHEN SHINE TOLD PEOPLE SHE BARTENDED AT THE BUCKHORN, their eyes widened. "What's a nice girl like you," they said, and then their voices trailed off. "I heard somebody got shot," they said. There was a real bullet hole in the mirror, but it was ancient history—part of the bar's character, like the heads on the walls and the smell of stale beer. To Shine, it felt safe, like sitting on a gargantuan comfy couch with all your cousins—sunk into the softness, everyone good-naturedly elbowing everyone else.

Not only that. As the bartender, Shine was the center of everything. She entertained the loners, introduced people, facilitated everyone's good time, and decided who stayed and who went. It was the next best thing to being on TV. Maybe someday she'd walk back through that door and everyone would whisper, "That's Shine. She used to work here."

Someday. Shine flipped a beer glass upside down and stuck it onto the brushes in the sink full of hot soapy water. She worked it up and down, rinsed it, then put it on the metal drain board. "Who's the most famous person who's come through that door?" she asked Doc, a forever regular who walked like a ship rolling on the high seas. Doc sat with his elbows resting on the edge of the bar, framing his draft of Bud.

"In the old days, this was a tent," Doc said, "and everybody stopped here because right out there was the railroad depot." He lifted his right elbow toward the tracks a half a block away. "Before they moved it on down."

"Even you weren't alive for that," One-ball Paul said. Paul stood watching the door, leaning with his back against the bar and his thin elbows hooked over the edge. Everybody knew he was waiting for Serita, only everybody also knew Serita was over at Coppers Corners with Lee Mangus, the UPS guy.

"I don't know," Shine said and winked at Doc. "I heard the reason Doc got his nickname was because he doctored up at Crow Agency when Custer had his last stand." The real reason Doc had his nickname was because he was a medic in Vietnam.

Doc's eyes squinted a smile. "The most famous person to walk through that door is going to be Shine."

"Yeah," Paul said. "She's going to replace Kathy Lee as America's top anchor, once she gets that TV degree."

Shine shook her head. "I'll be lucky to bring coffee to Geha over at KGWN in Cheyenne."

Doc shook his head and Paul turned around and looked at Shine. Paul said, "It's going to be you, Shine. You're beautiful and smart and … and …" He blushed and glanced at Doc. Doc was nodding his head.

"If Regis hits on you, pressures you, you let me know," Doc said, his face serious.

"Naw," Nance said and raised her head off the bar. Nance, who was married to Tommy Jon the trucker, was drunk on Gin

Rickeys. "That's Kelly what's-her-name. Kathy Lee hasn't been there for ages."

"We'll put your … Seven-Up can? … up there on the Wall of Fame," Paul said. The Wall of Fame was empty cans and bottles—Coors Light and Mickey's Big Mouth, McGillicuddy's and Jack Daniels Green Label—resting on little shelves with names on wooden plaques underneath them. They were tributes to regulars who had died.

As they talked, Shine watched a big man with a face like a boot walk along the sidewalk outside. He walked with his shoulders back but with his head curled forward like he was trying to be bigger and smaller at the same time. The door creaked as he pushed through. He stepped in and shrugged off his coat. The big man had arm muscles that strained the seams of his green long-sleeved t-shirt, and his waste narrowed as it disappeared into a pair of tan Carhart overalls. His face was broad and leathery brown with the prominent jaw that reminded Shine of a cartoon character.

Shine laughed and said to Doc and Paul, "You guys. If that happens, I'll drink Courvoisier." She turned and walked down the bar to take the big guy's order. The plastic mat squished under her feet, and her soles stuck and pulled with a k-k-k-k-k, k-k-k-k-k.

As he made his way to the bar, the big man craned his head to look at all the taxidermy mounts on the walls. The Buck was lined with the heads of buffalo, moose, elk, and antelope and full mounts of fish and fox and even a dwarf calf, but it was most famous for its full mount of a two-headed colt. The mounts always felt like blessings to Shine, like the spirits of all the people and animals were here in this room, looking after them—sort of like Noah's Ark, or Yoda and Obi Wan in the last of the first three Star Wars.

The big man pushed aside a stool with his thigh, put his meaty hands with black-rimmed fingernails spread-eagle on the bar, and lowered his head. His eyes were so pale they looked white, wide open and guileless like a child's.

"What can I get you?" Shine said.

"Fuzzy navel," the big man said.

Shine didn't react, even though he looked like a beer-and-shot-of-whiskey kind of guy. She nodded. In smooth motions, she scooped a tumbler full of ice from the well and poured the peach schnapps and the orange juice. She stuck in a straw. "That'll be three bucks," she said, as she placed the drink on a napkin in front of him.

The big man pulled a curled brown leather wallet on a chain from his back pocket and paid with a twenty. She took the bill and rang it up on the till and gave him his change. She nodded to him and then turned and walked back down the bar.

"I don't think it's right," Martin was saying from the end stool next to the wall. He was hunched over with his two-fingered hands cupping his beer glass. Martin came in every day shortly after four, right after his last class, and had exactly two pitchers of Coors Light—one he paid for and the second free because of Happy Hour. "Tug's last can fell down, and they didn't put it back up. They just stuck it up there." He nodded toward the Buckhorn beer can stuck under the bear trap on the high shelf above the bar. On the Wall of Fame where Tug's last can had rested now stood a picture of a young man in uniform with laughing eyes and a medal, a congressional gold star.

"Mo got that *Pulling a Marine* in Vietnam," Doc said, a growl in his voice.

"I'm not saying he shouldn't be up there too," Martin said. "I'm not saying that at all. But Tug died right here in the bar—heck, maybe on this stool—and he was way before Mo's time. His takes precedence."

Paul had turned back around and was watching the door again. "No," he said and pointed the other direction down the bar. "It was the fifth stool from that end."

"Shut the fuck up, Martin," Doc said.

Shine considered whether she should say anything. A good bartender keeps the peace, but you have to know when to step in and when it's best to let things be. Doc was a good guy, so generally he was unlikely to pursue things, but now he was a little drunk and they were talking about Vietnam. You had to watch yourself on that subject around Doc. Martin was a good guy too, a soft computer geek who loved science fiction and fantasy novels—he wasn't the confrontational type.

Shine decided it would peter out. With one ear on their discussion, Shine walked back down the bar to where the big guy sat. He'd left a tip on the inner rail, a fiver. Shine raised her eyebrows. She picked it up and put it in the tip jar. "Another?" she asked.

"Yeah," he said.

"What's your name?" Shine said as she made his drink.

"John."

"I'm Shine."

He raised his eyebrows.

"Short for Shineha," she said, "the sun in the Book of Abraham—my parents are hippies."

27

"Some people call me Big John, like the song."

"All right, Big John," Shine said.

He nodded to the long shelf above the bar. "That horse have two heads?" The two-headed colt lay on its belly with its eyes closed and its necks and legs splayed forward like it'd just been born. One head fanned up behind the other.

"Yeah," Shine said and placed the second drink in front of him. When he reached for his wallet, she said, "That's okay. It's free," and pointed to the Happy Hour sign.

"Is it real?" Big John said, looking at the colt.

"Yes," Shine said. At first, Shine had wondered, too, whether a clever taxidermist had created the creature, like putting spike deer horns on the head of a large jackrabbit to create the jackalope that was mounted among the plaques on the Wall of Fame. But the two-headed colt was real. It'd been born over by Wheatland. It'd lived, some people said, for a couple of weeks before it passed on. When it was born, both heads stuck out at the same time, and the vet was called because everybody thought the horse was having twins and they were caught shoulder to shoulder in the birth canal. When they pulled it out, though, there was only one body.

"The sad thing is," Shine said, "it couldn't eat. It couldn't coordinate its legs well enough to go to its mother to suck. Pretty much starved to death."

Shine thought she could still see the thinness of it under all that dust, the manginess of the hide from not eating, the expression on its face. She knew that the mount was largely the creation of the taxidermist. Still, it was all there, and it made her stomach upset if she thought about it.

"What'd the mother do?" Big John said. "Reject the freak?"

"The freak? Oh, the colt. No. In fact, she'd nudge it, trying to get it to latch on. She was all upset when they finally put it out of its misery."

"Most mothers would've given up on someone as fucked up as that."

"Aah," Shine said and nodded to him and then moved back down the bar.

Afternoon slipped toward evening. Most of the Happy Hour regulars were drunk on their stools and the bar was filling up with college kids and pool leaguers. Three college guys in low-slung dockers and layered t-shirts slouched in the corner booth and played quarters. There was the low hum of voices and the *kink!* of pool balls and every once in a while someone put money in the juke box. Neil, the other night bartender, clocked in. He was a stocky guy who had played football, and everybody called Armstrong because he had taken an astronomy class once.

Martin had gone home and Nance was propped in the corner of a booth passed out. Nance's husband Tommy Jon, still in dirty overalls, came in. Big John and Paul started talking, and then he, Doc, Paul, and Tommy Jon played pool up front because league had the table in the back.

Shine took a round of drinks out to them. Doc was saying to Tommy Jon, "You hear about that gal raped in the ally, right out the back door here?" He nodded. "Four in the morning."

Big John wasn't saying anything, but his head was cocked to the side and his forehead was bunched up. Shine couldn't read his expression.

"Someone was raped?" Tommy Jon said.

"Yep," Doc said, "Skinny Marie. After, they had to pull her out of the dumpster, half-frozen and hysterical."

Shine pulled the empty drink tray to her chest. Before the rape, the alley hadn't bothered Shine at all, but now when she took the garbage out, even in broad daylight, she kept her eyes open, her body tense. She glanced over to Big John. There was something about his presence—solid as the immense granite boulders up at Vedauwoo—that made her feel better, safer.

"Cattle Kate took her home, I heard," Shine said.

"Somebody said they were college boys," Doc continued, "but I don't think so. That time of night, college boys are drunk off their asses passed out at home."

Shine glanced over at the three college guys in the booth. Their heads were together, and they were talking rapid-fire in low voices.

"Could be a drifter, someone coming through with the railroad," Paul said.

"People don't do that anymore," Tommy Jon said. "Ride the rails."

"Do too," Big John said. "I ran from Albuquerque to Denver one time a couple of years ago." He handed Shine a fifty for the drinks. She went behind the bar and rang it up and brought back the change. He nodded to her and gave her a twenty for a tip. She smiled and nodded to him in thanks. He smiled back and she thought he even blushed a little.

"It wasn't in the paper. Rapes, things like that never get in the papers," Paul said. "I personally saw a guy shot and killed in those trailers out on 230. Not a peep. Might as well not've happened."

"Well," Shine said, "did you tell them it happened? How're they going to report it if no one tells them?"

Paul shook his head. "I'm not going to be the one." He looked at Doc, who shrugged.

"That was meth, I heard," Doc said.

"Meth?" Big John said.

Doc nodded.

"Naw," Tommy Jon said. "That was what's-her-name, sleeping with her husband's best friend. Don't you remember? She was a fat chick who never took a bath. You remember."

"I was there," Paul said. "Weren't no fat chick. I'm not denying anything else."

Shine turned to go back to the bar.

"Speaking as a member of the medical profession," Doc said, a smirk on his face, "that stuff'll kill you."

"Live fast and die young, I always say," Shine heard Paul say as she went behind the bar.

Doc, Paul, Tommy Jon, and Big John continued playing pool till the night wound down. Right before last call, Tommy Jon warmed up his car and then woke Nance up and helped her out to it. Shine was wiping down tables when Doc left, drunk and rolling like an ocean. "Shine on," he said and cackled. When Armstrong called last call at two, Paul and Big John were sitting on stools, their heads bent together, talking. Big John caught Shine's eye and pointed to their shot glasses. Shine pulled the Yukon Jack from the back bar and filled them. They drank them down and then got up together to leave. Big John tucked a tip on the back of the bar as he left, saying, "Pretty lady."

Shine and Armstrong closed up. Shine wiped down the bar while Armstrong brought up beer from downstairs to stock the cooler. As she swiped by, she picked up Big John's tip. It was a one hundred dollar bill. She looked up to the door and held up the bill. No one was there. She hesitated for a minute and then pocketed the bill.

Her first thought was, now I can pay off that credit card! Her second thought was, I shouldn't take this. Her third thought was, where did he get the money to tip like that? Her fourth thought was, is he going to want anything in return?

The next day, Paul and Big John came in at three thirty. They looked like they hadn't slept but they were in good spirits. They came up to the bar and ordered. Paul ordered a Pabst and a shot of Yukon, and Big John ordered a fuzzy navel.

"Sweeten your disposition?" Paul said.

"Damn straight," Big John said.

"Spent the night together, did you?" Shine said as she made the drinks.

Paul made a comic sheepish face and pulled his shoulders up to his ears. "Saw the sun rise, didn't we, honey?" he said.

Big John didn't say anything.

Shine set the drinks in front of them. When Big John started to pay, Shine looked into his eyes and smiled and shook her head. He smiled and nodded. When Paul went to the bathroom, Shine ducked into the back room and grabbed the plate of chocolate chip cookies she'd baked that morning. She put them in front of Big John. "Thanks," she said.

He shrugged and eyed the cookies.

"These are my dad's recipe," she said. "He's the best cook." She leaned forward and rested her forearms on the bar. "Try one."

Using his fingertips, he tried to pull the cellophane off the plate. It stuck tight. Shine reached forward to help him. She said, "Here, let—" He jerked back and brushed her hands. The edges of his fingers rasped Shine's palm like warm sandpaper. He took a step back. Shine felt herself redden but she reached forward and yanked the cellophane open. It ripped and then stretched into a long ribbon. She held the plate out to him.

He took a step forward and then gently pulled a cookie from the plate. He closed his eyes and took a bite. He chewed and swallowed and opened his eyes. Then he nodded his head. "Thank you, Shine," he said. When he said her name, it sounded of the south, like he was saying *moonshine*. Shine set the plate in front of him and stepped back from the bar.

Without saying anything, Big John unbuttoned the right sleeve of his yellow and green plaid flannel shirt and slowly rolled it up his arm, making sure the folds were straight. When it was past the elbow he pushed it up to his armpit. It took some doing because his biceps were so big they strained the shirt material.

Then he held out his arm. His biceps were huge. They looked like Arnold Schwarzenegger's in *Conan*. The veins bulged blue and the muscles were like smooth stones under the skin, which was marred with an angry slantwise patch down the side of his arm—a wide ropelike ridge, four inches long and an inch wide. It was paler than the surrounding skin and protruded like cancer.

"My dad took a chainsaw to me when I was twelve," Big John said. There was no expression on his face. He didn't eye her face for a reaction. He didn't avoid her eyes like he was ashamed. It was just a fact.

Involuntarily, Shine's arms folded across her body. "That's awful," Shine said, trying to keep the intenseness of her emotion out of her voice.

"Is it?" he said. He rolled his sleeve back down.

"Well, I made you these cookies," she said. She looked from his arm to the plate of cookies and then back to his face. She fought an impulse to grab back the plate of cookies and hug them to her chest.

Paul returned from the bathroom. "What's this?" he said.

Big John put his palm on top of the plate of cookies.

Paul looked at Shine.

Shine shrugged. "I made cookies," she said.

"Can I have one?" Paul said.

"They're John's," Shine said. She looked at him and raised her eyebrows. "Can he have one?"

Big John let his hand rest on top of the cookies and then slowly pulled it back. "Sure," he said.

"Thanks," Paul said and grabbed a cookie from the pile and took a big bite. "Yum," he said and took a drink of his Pabst. He looked at Big John. "What makes you so special? She's never baked cookies for me."

"My sweet disposition," John said.

Big John and Paul left shortly after. Big John held the cookies close to his body as he left.

Shine couldn't get the image of that angry welt out of her mind. Proud flesh, her mom called it. Shine had always thought

34

it meant you could brag about your scars, but now she wasn't so sure. Big John hadn't bragged. It was fact. Had it gone so deep, he didn't even realize what it meant? Was the violence down there, not just on him but in him too?

The next day, Shine called Cattle Kate to cover for her, claiming cramps, but Friday Shine had to go in because Kate always went to the Moose on Fridays for prime rib and hell would freeze over before Kate missed that.

It was cold. Shine's breath was ghost white as she pushed at the Buck's door. It stuck for a minute, and she had to plant both her feet and push with both gloved hands to get it open. It groaned as it scraped across the floor. As she stepped in, heat blasted her face and the smell enveloped her—piss and vomit and piney cleaning fluid, and under that something wild and earthy. She stopped and looked around. Big John wasn't there—thank goodness, she thought—still, though, something wasn't right. Call it bartender's intuition. The people were edgy—she could feel it. Was it a full moon? Every bartender knows to watch for the full moon.

Armstrong was on his knees by the radiator with a bucket and some rags.

"What's up?" Shine said.

"Nance puked her nachos," Armstrong said.

"I'm sorry," Shine said.

"The humidity," Armstrong said and smiled. "It's not you."

"What?"

"The door. It makes the door stick."

"Oh, yeah," Shine said and walked behind the bar.

Doc was there, a pitcher in front of him. "What's the matter?" Doc said, "You ain't got your usual shine."

Shine shrugged and went down the bar to clock in.

As the night wore on, Shine kept her eye on the door. Big John wasn't there for Happy Hour, and he wasn't there later when Paul got mouthy with Armstrong and got eighty-sixed for life for the hundredth time. He wasn't there when Nance started crying on her stool and was helped to the bathroom by Constance, who had a beautiful body but a face like a brick.

If John came in, Shine told herself, she'd treat him with respect but be distant. She'd discourage him, if he did have any ideas. He couldn't buy her. She had no obligation to him. He gave the money of his own free will, and she took it, but nothing was agreed. It wasn't a transaction. She did not feel guilty.

About one in the morning, things started to wind down. People were leaving. An older guy was in a booth in the back necking with Constance. Doc had gotten drunk, passed out, woken up, went to the bathroom, eaten a hot dog, and was sober again.

Shine leaned into the cooler to get a beer. There was a loud rattling *bang!* Shine pushed herself up in time to see the door wide open and rebounding from the wall and Big John hurling across the room knocking over tables and chairs.

Armstrong can't handle him, Shine thought, even if he used to play football. She whirled and ran down to the gate by the end of the bar and grabbed the baseball bat that was propped there in case of emergency. She looked up in time to see Armstrong standing with one arm up and one arm out like he was a policeman directing traffic.

Big John jerked to a stop and then stood swaying. His mouth hung open and spit dribbled down his chin. His eyes were wide and rolling in the sockets. "Uuuuunnnnhh," he said.

Is he on something? Does meth do that? Cocaine?

"Call the cops," Armstrong said over his shoulder.

"Nnnnnnnnnnnnh," Big John said. He never closed his mouth, just stood drooling. Then he looked at Shine. His eyes were pools of water that began to seep down his face. "Aaaaah," he said.

Doc said something.

"What?" Armstrong said.

"His jaw's broken," Doc said. "Fucking hanging by the skin."

Then Shine saw the red starting to shade to purple on Big John's huge jaw. She saw the spit was mingled with blood. "Shit," Shine said and dropped the bat. She sprinted down the bar and dialed 911.

There was a pause on the line and then the dispatcher picked up. "What is the nature of your emergency?" the woman said.

"It's Shine at the Buckhorn. John, a guy, he's been hurt. Someone here, a doctor, thinks his jaw's broken."

"Is there an altercation in progress?"

"No. It happened—I don't know—outside, I think."

There was a pause. "Police officers are on their way. I'll send an ambulance too."

"Thanks. Thank you," Shine said.

"Please stay on the line so I can get your information," the dispatcher said.

Shine hesitated. Her first impulse was to withhold the information, as if not telling would pull her out of the situation. She felt guilty, dirty. With the palm of her free hand, she rubbed the skin on the arm that held the phone. Then she gave her name and home phone number.

As Shine talked, Armstrong and Doc each took one of Big John's arms and pulled him down into a chair. Then Armstrong came behind the bar and filled a bar rag with ice and walked back around. He tried to put it on John's jaw, but John batted it away. All the while, Doc sat in a chair next to John and talked into his ear. Shine saw the look in Doc's eyes—he'd been there before and he knew what he was doing. This somehow made Shine feel a little better.

Within three minutes, police cars pulled up out front and three cops came in, their hands on their belts, their chests puffed out, and their voices deep. After they looked at John and talked with Doc, two of them ran out the door and down the street toward the railroad tracks. An ambulance pulled up and two EMTs came in with a trolley. John refused to be put on the stretcher, so the cop and one of the EMTs took his arms and walked him out to the ambulance. The last Shine saw of Big John was his bulging arms as he pulled himself into the ambulance.

All of a sudden, Shine felt weak. Only then did she realize the adrenalin shooting through her. She took a deep breath.

Armstrong gave last call, and then fifteen minutes later, just as Shine and Armstrong pushed everyone out the door, Paul pushed in through the door. "I saw 'em," he said. "All three of them had pipes—I saw 'em. They had big-ass pipes. They really did." Paul had followed the cops as they ran down to the

38

tracks and found the three college guys with pipes. One guy confessed right away that they'd jumped Big John and beat him. Not for money, he'd said. They were just messing around.

Just messing around? Big John standing there, his face wild and open like a child's, and they'd just been messing around.

Soon the bar was empty and the door was locked and it was just her and Armstrong to close up. "Well," Armstrong said, letting the word hang in the air, as he went to the basement to get cases of beer.

After he'd gone, Shine slumped into the bar. She was so exposed, standing there. Anyone could see her pale face glowing through those huge windows, its dangerous shine. The bullet hole in the mirror—that's how he'd done it. The guy was jealous of a woman, so he hid in the alley across the street with a thirty-aught-six and shot into the bar full of people. Anybody could be there right now, watching her, and she wouldn't know it. She glanced up at the walls and the taxidermy mounts. There was something she hadn't noticed before—age had pulled the animals' lips back from their shiny teeth. They were all staring at her and snarling.

Mouse

I GREW UP ON A FARM IN CENTRAL WYOMING with just my dad and a hired hand named Clay. I have no memories of my mother, who ran away with a man from Last Chance shortly after I was born. I may have missed the idea of her growing up, but I didn't miss her.

But that's not what this story is about.

Every spring we had to clean the irrigation ditches to get ready to flood them. They'd been dry all winter and were choked with last season's blown-in dry weeds and desiccated water-made dams. To clean ditches, you take a fork that looks like a large hoe except, instead of a flat blade, four large tines extend out and then down so you can hook out the debris. You have to walk the ditches for miles, and by the end of the day, your shoulders ache from the yank and lift, and the soles of your feet are numb from treading on stones.

I was ten years old, and today was the day. My small morning-lit bedroom was behind the kitchen, and I woke to the smell of coffee and bacon and the popping of frying eggs.

"Mouse," Papa called from the kitchen, "pony up."

Papa was not a tall man, but he was broad without being fat. He had smile-worn grooves on his cheeks and around his eyes, and the back of his neck looked like elephant skin. When

I was little and we went into Last Chance for parts or groceries, he always held my hand fiercely—being country-raised, I didn't have the proper fear of cars, and his usual gentleness didn't translate to hand-holding.

That day, I wanted to sleep in. Course, I always wanted to sleep in as a kid, but Saturdays were work days, and Papa always saved those jobs we did together for Saturdays. With only Clay to help, there was always work to be done. Papa wasn't the yelling type—all it took was that tightening in his shoulders and I knew I'd disappointed him. It devastated me to disappoint him. So I pushed back the covers and put my feet on the cold wood floor. I pulled on my oldest flared jeans with a hole in one knee, my favorite Josie and the Pussycats t-shirt, a gray hooded sweatshirt, and an old pair of pink canvas tennis shoes.

As I came into the kitchen, Papa, with a threadbare kitchen towel tied over his tan Carhart bibs, scooped eggs from the frying pan and shoveled them onto a plate. They were just the way I liked them—looking at you, but crispy brown around the edges to where they crunched in your teeth. I eyed the eggs. Then I pulled dishes from the cupboard and set the table just as Clay came in from letting the chickens out of the coop, slopping the hogs, feeding the dogs, all those chores. He smelled of chicken manure and shaving cream. He placed a small bucket of white-, brown-, and green-shelled eggs on the counter.

Clay was a sandy-haired slouched-over young man who'd been written off by his relatives, so he came to live with us. Papa knew him before from the sale barn, where Clay ran livestock down the alleys and worked in the kitchen for pocket money. One day, Papa asked him if he was available to help clean out the barn. They dropped him off at the end of drive just like a stray mutt, and he'd been with us ever since.

As Clay stood at the sink and washed his hands, he said over his shoulder, "Hey, Mouse. How's the girly girl?" which was what he always said by way of greeting.

"I'm an honorary boy," I said and grinned.

"You can tell by the hair growing on her chest," Papa said to Clay as he sat down.

We ate. I put away extra that day because the eggs were so good sopped in toast. Papa smiled at me in approval.

After breakfast, I went with Papa to feed the bum calves. Everyone knew Papa would take calves who'd been abandoned by their mothers or whose mothers had died, so all the farms and ranches that didn't want to bother with them sold them to us cheap. Papa fed them up for a year or two and then sold them, another way to make a few dollars. To suckle them, we had two milk cows, Texas and Elizabeth. Texas was a black and white Holstein with a patch on her right side that approximated the shape of that state. Elizabeth was a Jersey, with the coloring of a Siamese cat. Elizabeth was as gentle as could be and readily accepted the calves. Texas, though, wasn't so easy.

Breath coming white in the morning chill, we stepped from the bright slanting light into the barn, and it took a minute for our eyes to adjust. The barn smelled pleasantly of fresh cow manure and timothy and old wood warming in the sun. One of the cows lowed to us. Their bags were full, stretched round and tight from the night, and they were ready for relief. Their heads hung over the fence and into the alley, and we snapped lead ropes to their halters and led them out their gate and into the pen that held the five bums. The calves were on them as soon as we came in, sticking their noses up into the cows' groins and latching on to the teats. I had Elizabeth, and all I had to do was stand in the center of the pen holding the lead rope and she stood there belching and chewing over last night's grain. The calves jostled each other and wiggled their tails, and every once in a while one would pull back and bunt Elizabeth's bag, prompting her to let her milk down.

As I said, Texas wasn't so easy. Papa slipped a rope over the halter and around her neck up next to the ears and snugged her to a corner post. Then he snagged the leather quirt hanging from a high nail and stood up next to her head and talked to her. "Now, girl, keep it steady. Whoa, girl. They ain't a hurting you." The two bums crowded up shoulder to shoulder and tried to latch on. One of them couldn't quite get its mouth around the swollen teat, so Papa bent over and gently pulled its lower jaw forward and open and inserted the teat. The calf got the hang of it and then pushed forward and suckled. As Papa stepped back, Texas kicked her hind leg up to try to dislodge the calves. "Now what'd you go and do that for?" Papa said in his even voice and flipped the quirt up against Texas's flanks, popping the end. "This ain't your idea I know, but we're going to make it your idea. Them little ones are harmless and they need you now more than ever." Texas's skin wiggled there where the leather landed as if trying to dislodge a fly. She started to kick again, and Papa popped her again, harder this time. I could hear the hollow striking of the quirt. Texas flinched and then stood, accepting the calves.

Once that was done, we set about cleaning ditches. We dropped Clay off on Long Ditch, which skirted the valley for miles. Dad dropped me off on a shorter ditch that wound down among hardpan and fields, through stands of cottonwoods, and under roads. Then he drove to another ditch that started near where Clay would end up. That way, Clay could pick up the truck and drive to pick us up.

"Got your lunch?" Papa said as I pushed open the door. I nodded. In the bag hung across my chest, I had yesterday's pancakes rolled with butter and sugar and wrapped in wax paper and water in a plastic bottle. "Watch out for snakes," he called as I started down the ditch. And so I made my way, humming and forking weeds.

Toward the end of the day, under the spring-budded limbs of a small cottonwood, in among the water-bared roots, I pulled a matted clump of gray leaves, and with it the fur-lined nest of a mouse. What I noticed first was pink. There was bright pink in among the gray of the rocks and the gray of the roots and the gray of the dirt. Bright pink, like you'd find in a set of crayons. I knelt and leaned in, one hand braced on the propped fork. There were four baby mice, one slightly bigger than the other three. They looked like they were made of rubber. They were pink through and through, with touches of gray on their backs and over their bulbous eyes, which had not yet opened. With the rush of cold, they made squeaking noises at the edge of hearing and waved their stump legs.

So I did the only logical thing: I rescued them. I wrapped them in the fur from their nest and tucked them into my pocket. I hefted the fork and finished the ditch, every once in a while

45

peeking anxiously at the tiny bodies. I needn't've worried—with the heat of my body, they soon settled and slept.

I didn't tell Papa and Clay when they picked me up.

"How'd it go?" Papa said as I clambered onto the middle of the bench seat and Clay got in the passenger side and pulled the door shut. I sucked in a deep breath. It felt good to be sitting, and the smell of men's sweat filled the cab.

"Fine," I said.

"Did you have any trouble?"

I shook my head.

When we got home, I stashed the mice in a box and put them behind the couch near a heat register.

Throughout the supper of hamburger steaks and fried greens with bacon, I tried to reason out what I might feed them. We didn't have any cow's milk because all the milk was going to the bum calves. And of course we didn't buy milk. But we did have canned milk and powdered milk. I chose the canned milk but thought it was probably too thick, so I'd water it down. But that might take away what the mice needed, so I decided to add sugar to give it that extra boost. Not too much, but a bit to help them along.

"Awful quiet, Mouse," Papa said when supper was over.

"Cat got her tongue," Clay said and pretended to try to grab for it.

After dinner, Papa and Clay listened to a University of Wyoming basketball game through the hissing and crackling of the radio, and I fiddled in the kitchen. After they'd gone to bed—Papa saying, "Don't be long"—I pulled the mice from their warm nook. I keyed open a can of milk and carefully poured a good half-inch into a small bowl. I let the tap run into it for a short second and then spooned in one, two, three teaspoons of sugar. Way too much liquid for their tiny bellies, I knew, but I had to start somewhere. I stirred and stirred until I couldn't feel any grains on the bottom of the bowl. I stuck my finger into it and then brought it to my tongue and swallowed. It was sweet. I retrieved a syringe from the refrigerator, where we kept it next to the calf vaccinations. I dunked the tip into the milk and pulled back the plunger, and the off-white liquid filled the tube. Then I gently pulled away the fur tuft to reveal the tiny pink bodies.

I chose the largest one first. I gently picked it up by the scruff and then palmed it. The pink body squirmed and struggled. I cupped my hand to support the body, placed the tip of the syringe tight against the almost invisible lips, and pressed the plunger. The mouse baby first struggled to pull back, but the instant the milk hit its lips its jaw worked and worked and it lapped like a dog and chewed on the end of the syringe and suckled. I repeated it with all four babies. Then they were content and slept. I placed the milk in the fridge for later, taking one more glance at them next to the heat register before I went to bed.

Early the next morning, as I fed them for third time, I felt someone standing at the door behind me. I jumped but then tried to act like it was nothing. I tossed the one in my hand into the box along with the syringe and blocked the box with my body and quickly threw over a towel over it. Then I started singing the song I used to sing to my dollies: "Lollipop, lollipop, oh lolly lolly lolly."

"Up early," came Papa's voice.

"I wanted to make my dolly breakfast," I said in a fake voice.

I turned to look at him. His eyebrows were lifted but he was smiling. "You haven't played with dolls in years," he said and walked closer. "Let me see."

"She's sleeping," I said frantically. "You'll wake her."

He reached and flipped back the towel. I knew better than to try to stop him. His smile froze on his face. He looked at them for a long time. His shoulders tightened, and in response my body shot through with adrenalin and made my hands shake. I'd disappointed him.

"Oh, baby," he said and slowly sat in a chair.

"I'll take good care of them," I said. "You won't even be bothered." Then I remembered school and who would feed them while I was at school? Maybe I could get Clay to help. And it wouldn't be long before they were big enough not to have to be fed all the time. "Can I keep them?" I said.

He didn't answer for a long time and just looked at them. Then he looked at me all scary tender and said, "There are some things you won't understand. I could try to tell you why, but you wouldn't understand. So you have to trust me. They're baby mice. They're going to die—if not now, soon. You've got to kill them."

I don't know the look on my face, but when he saw it his jaw hardened and he said, "Just do it, Annie," and turned to make breakfast.

I looked at the mice and I looked at Papa's back. All kinds of arguments rose in my mind—they'll do just fine, they only need a little food and a warm place, I can take care of them, their mother wouldn't come back to the nest after it was destroyed, and besides the water would fill the ditch anyway, washing it all away, I had to rescue them, hadn't I? I looked at the tightness in Papa's shoulders. He didn't reach to turn on the radio like he often did on Sunday mornings. I looked at the mice. The big one and two of the small ones were curled together asleep, and other one was propped up on its front legs, trying to walk, its head bobbing up and down. I reached out and ran my finger down its head.

I looked at Papa again. Why did I have to do this? Why? It wasn't about whether I could take care of them, and it wasn't about the fact that they were mice that ate grain and chewed through things. It was something else, something bigger than all that. The way he'd given me that stricken look, and then how he'd hardened. It was something I didn't understand, but it had to be done. I felt my throat close a little. It wasn't a choice thing.

So I did it. I picked up them up and took them outside. I found a big flat rock and set them down. The wind was whipping my hair into my eyes and I kept trying to flip it over my shoulder but it wouldn't stay but instead stuck to my eyelashes and the wetness of my mouth and I tried to spit to clear it. There was the rushing sound of the wind through the reaching branches of the cottonwoods—a sound which, if you listened hard enough, you could hear the individual leaves as they batted against each other. There was the tinny smell that preceded rain.

Near the flat rock, I found another rock that was round and heavy. It was small enough to hold in one hand. I did a test run. I lifted the rock above my head and brought it down hard onto the flat stone. Chink. In the process, I pinched my thumb. Just sharp pressure at first and then the pain throbbed through. I dropped the rock. Blood oozed from the ripped skin next to my thumbnail. I put the thumb into my mouth and sucked. There was the metallic taste of blood. I felt my sinuses swell, tears starting at inner corners of my eyes, so I pulled the thumb from my mouth and bit my tongue to keep from bawling.

I reached in and picked up a pink mouse, one of the smaller three that I couldn't tell apart. I placed it on the flat rock. Then I picked up the smaller rock with both hands and positioned it so that my fingertips were well back, so much I was afraid I'd drop it. I pulled it high above my head and back so gravity helped keep it in my hands. I looked at the pink body there on the rock. It had rolled onto its belly and was struggling ineffectually to rise to its feet and moving its head back and forth, back and forth. It wobbled and fell onto its side, and so, then, I brought down the rock.

Maybe I was tentative because I'd rapped my thumb. Maybe I was tentative because I didn't want to do it. Maybe I just wanted to cause less pain. Whatever the reason, the first blow didn't kill it, and it let out a high-pitched squeal that went on and on and didn't seem to pause for breath. When I pulled back, it writhed. So I didn't even raise the rock this time; I set it squarely onto the mouse's head and ground down with all my weight until the noise stopped.

Then I tossed away the smaller rock. For the other three, I placed the heel of my shoe gently and squarely onto their skulls and, without lifting, shifted my weight decisively onto that side and felt the bones as they crunched underfoot. There was no sound this way. I saved the big one for last, and his skull was stronger and felt like a pebble at first before it gave way. Then

I stepped away and rasped the soles of my shoes on the ground, kicking and scuffing.

Clay came outside in his stocken feet and walked over to me. He glanced at the flat rock and the box and then knelt down in front of me. He didn't say anything but reached out his warm hands to envelope my shoulders. He looked at my face. He didn't smile or frown—he was totally focused on me. Thoughts shifted behind his eyes, and his face made small adjustments. Then he shook his head slightly, squeezed my shoulders, and stood.

"Girly-girl," he whispered and took my hand to lead me back to the house.

But I shook him off and turned away, and I heard the soft pad of his footfalls recede. I stayed there for a long time listening to the wind moaning in the trees.

Oranges

THE TRAILER DOOR WOULDN'T STAY SHUT because the latch was broken, so the blue-black houseflies buzzed around the sink full of dirty dishes that smelled of rotten fruit and soured milk.

On the linoleum floor next to the sink, Tamsen crouched with her bare knees up under her dress and laid down a frayed pink hand towel and smoothed out the wrinkles with her palms. In a stained t-shirt, Parker stood in the doorway and watched her with his hands tucked into the corners of his diaper. Parker's eyes followed Tamsen as she scooted a chair across the floor and next to the counter. She climbed up on the chair and on tippytoes pulled two plastic plates from the bottom shelf of the upper cupboard and held them to her chest with one arm as she climbed off the chair. She put them down on the hand towel, one on each end, and then straightened and impatiently flipped her long brown hair back over her shoulder. She walked back and climbed up the chair. She reached for the second shelf for the plastic cups but couldn't reach, so she got down, moved the chair, and pulled two plastic cups from the sink and turned on the water and rinsed them. A cloud of flies rose and hovered. She got down and put the cups dripping wet on the towel. Then she went to the silverware drawer and got a fork and a plastic spoon. She placed the fork next to one plate and the plastic spoon next to the other.

Tamsen walked over to Parker and grasped his arm and led him over next the plate with the plastic spoon. She walked around behind him and placed a hand on each shoulder and pressed down. He swayed a minute before bending down with one hand and lowering himself to the floor.

"Cold, Tam'en," he said and drew his legs up to his chest. He wrapped his arms around his legs and held on to each elbow.

"If you'd keep your pants on," Tamsen said. She turned and walked across the linoleum and into the living room. The trailer's floor complained as she crossed over the spot under the trailer where she took Parker when Mama came home early or when she came home late, when they had to play like mice. Tamsen pulled the baby blanket off the couch and took it into the kitchen. She spread it out next to Parker and the hand towel. She walked around behind him and hooked her fingers under his armpits and lifted, grunting with the effort. He relaxed and let himself be lifted.

"Hot dogs?" Parker said. "Keek-up?"

"We'll see," Tamsen said.

She nudged him sideways onto the blanket and held his arm as he sat with his legs poking out in front of him. His legs pushed the hand towel sideways, and the dishes and silverware gave a dull rattle as they tumbled into a pile.

Tamsen gave an exaggerated sigh. She leaned over and pulled the towel out straight and rearranged the dishes.

Then Tamsen walked over to the olive-green refrigerator and pulled on the handle with her right hand. It didn't move.

Tamsen grasp it with both hands and bent her knees and let her weight drop. She hung from the handle and, first one and then the other, propped the soles of her baby blue flip-flops against the plastic grill under the door. Then she pulled. She arched her back and pulled her shoulders back like those pretty girls did on TV when they did cartwheels and flips. Tamsen pulled and pulled. The strap on her left flip-flop gave and her toes turned in and her ankle twisted and her knees bent. She arced sideways and her body slammed into the fridge door, knocking the two letter magnets onto the floor. Then her body swayed back to center and she hung from her right arm, her knees in a puddle underneath her.

"Fuck," she said.

"Quack, quack," Parker said. "Quack."

Tamsen lifted her right knee and placed her flip-flop sole flat on the floor. She lifted her left knee and tried to place her left sole, but the flip-flop hung sideways from her big toe and twisted her ankle as her weight came down. Tamsen stood for a minute and then took a step back from the fridge and turned toward the back hall. As hard as she could, she kicked her left foot. The flip-flop twisted as it came off her big toe and flipped up, twirling, and flew up and over. It landed among the empty bottles that lined the counter, bottles that had been full of Mama's juice. The bottles clinked as they jostled apart. One teetered before slowly tipping over into the sink, crashing in among the dirty dishes, shooing up another small cloud of flies.

Tamsen breathed in deeply and then pushed the air out all at once. She pulled her foot out of her other flip-flop and turned to Parker. "Parkie?" His eyes were wide and focused on the sink. He looked over to her. "No hot dogs," she said.

"Hot dog?" Parker said. "Keek-up?"

"No," Tamsen said. Then she turned to look at the kitchen. On top of the fridge was a plastic net of oranges. She considered them. They weren't supposed to eat them. Last week, Tamsen had been trying to peel an orange when Mama jerked it from her hand and threw it against the wall with a dull thump, juice splaying wide across the wall like a drawing of sunbeams. "Keep you fuckin' paws off," Mama had said before she went back to her bedroom to take a nap.

Tamsen looked from the oranges to Parker and then back to the oranges. She stood for a minute considering before she nodded her head and moved the chair from the sink to in front of the refrigerator. She climbed up on the chair and reached and reached but she could not reach the top of the fridge. Carefully, she bent her legs and then jumped. Her hands almost reached the top of the fridge, but when she came down, her foot slipped and she landed sideways on her butt bone on the chair. She clutched at the chair back and just managed to stay on the seat. She sat for a moment, breathing, and then climbed off the chair.

Limping, Tamsen moved over to the tall cupboard and pulled it open. The shelves were bare except for a wrinkled package of ramen noodles in pink cellophane and a rusted steel can without a label.

"Cookie?" Parker said.

Tamsen kept her back to him. She reached and fingered the cellophane and then with both hands picked up the can. She walked along the counter and set the can on floor next to the big wide drawer.

"No!" Parker said. He pointed back to the tall cupboard.

"No cookies, Parkie," she said. "We ate those last night." They had been stale, but Tamsen had felt lucky to find them stashed in a box by Mama's bed.

"Cookies," Parker said.

Tamsen opened the drawer and retrieved the can opener. She crouched down and curled forward so that her chest pressed against her knees. A hand on each handle, she opened the can opener wide and placed the little round blade on the lip of the can. Then, hunching her shoulders, she pushed the handles back together, grunting with the effort. When the handles were together, she grasped them with her left hand, which splayed wide in order to wrap around them, and with her right she turned the handle.

It was difficult at first. She pulled and pushed so hard the can ended up sideways on the floor. Using the handle, she picked it up again and sat it upright. This time, it worked. The handle turned easily.

Tamsen twisted and twisted, and slowly the can opener made its way around the lip. Finally, it went *clink* as the cut caught up with its beginning. Tamsen stopped and using both hands pulled open the can opener and placed it beside her on the floor. Using her index finger, she poked at the round metal of the detached lid. It didn't move. Tamsen picked up the can opener and brought it up above her head and then back down. She aimed it at the can. *Tang!* The can opener connected with the can and sent it rolling across the floor, the round disk of the lid separating and weaving its drunken way across the floor before falling over *plink!* in front of the fridge.

Tamsen pushed herself up and trotted over to the can that had stopped in the middle of the floor. She reached down and grabbed it and set it back upright. Nothing had leaked out of it. It was all in the can.

Something smelled though. At first it smelled sour like day-old milk, then it smelled like the pile of Parker's pajamas and Tamsen's dresses and Mama's underwear in the hall before Mama got around to washing. The really bad pile, after Tamsen had picked out all the ones that weren't so bad and worn them or put them back on Parker.

Tamsen peered into the can. Whatever had been in there was brown. Now it was a solid mass with cracks through it, and it was covered with a thick white film. Just to make sure, Tamsen sniffed it again. Yep, it was icky.

Then Parker was right behind her reaching around her for the can. She slapped his hand away. "No Parker! Bad," she said.

Parker pulled his arm back and his head bent forward. His cheeks turned red as he screwed up his face and tears seeped from his eyes, but he didn't make a sound. He just turned and shuffled toward the back hall.

Tamsen pushed up and went to him and wrapped her arms around him from behind. "It's okay," she said. He pulled for a minute and then slumped back against her.

Just then they heard a car pull into the driveway. They both froze and turned their heads to listen. Here's what they did not hear. They did not hear the gravel scrape under the tires as the car jerked to a halt. The car door didn't slam. There were no voices, no singing, so low angry mumbling. The footsteps on the treads were regular and light.

"Run!" Tamsen whispered and shoved Parker down the hall. He stumbled forward, so Tamsen wrapped her left arm around his ribs and pulled him along beside her. She pulled him through the first door they came to, the bathroom. "Shshsh," she said as Parker turned toward her with wide eyes.

There was no knock. The door opened and then shut. The floor creaked. Something was set on the table with a rustle of paper, a small thump, and the rattle of keys.

Parker stepped closer to Tamsen, and Tamsen put her hand on his arm. She kept her head cocked, listening.

"Parker, honey? Tamsen?" came the voice down the hall. It was Mama.

Neither Tamsen or Parker moved. They just looked at each other.

"Are you hungry, kiddos?" Mama said. "I brought Mickey Dees."

Parker hesitated just a second longer and then pushed past Tamsen. Tamsen grabbed at his shirt as he passed. "No, Parkie!" she said, but he twisted out of her grasp and went down the hall without looking back.

Tamsen didn't hesitate. She pushed out into the hall and sprinted, pushing past and in front of Parker as he entered the kitchen. She stopped. He bumped into her and she put her arms out behind herself and held him to her back.

The kitchen was filled with the golden smell of French fries. Liquid gushed from under Tamsen's tongue and filled her mouth. Her eyes focused on the bag, with its red and yellow logo, its top crumpled together like a present from Mama's hand. Tamsen wanted to go to the bag and rip it open and stuff French fries into her mouth. She could taste the salty oil and feel the crisp pressure of the ends and the soft bland mush of the centers.

She looked at Mama, keeping her arms behind her on either side of Parker. She kept shifting, keeping herself between Parker and Mama as Parker tried to squirm around her. She closed her mouth and took in a deep breath through her nose, sniffing. She couldn't smell any orange juice or cigarettes. When Mama came home late, she often smelled of orange juice and cigarettes.

"Tamsen, honey, there you are," Mama said. "Parker?" Mama craned her head, her eyes focusing down at Tamsen's body.

Tamsen stood, not saying anything.

"Mickey," Parker said.

Mama looked at them for a long minute and then turned to the bag and started pulling things out of it—paper-wrapped sandwiches, mounded boxes of French fries, cups of soda.

"You'll never guess what happened today," Mama said. "I got a job."

Parker finally managed to push around Tamsen. He rushed forward and then stopped at arm's reach away from Mama and looked up at her.

Mama stepped forward and crouched down and put her arms around him. He wrapped both of his around her neck, his head disappearing in her frizzy waves of red-orange hair. Then Mama looked at Tamsen.

"Do you know what that means?" Mama said.

Tamsen pulled in her chin and let her eyes drop to the floor.

"Do you know what that means, sweetie?"

Tamsen shook her head once, twice, in small motions.

"It means Mama'll be home more. It means we get more Mickey Dees." She pulled Parker away from her, wincing as

Parker pulled her hair in an effort to stay at her neck. She looked at him. "You'd like more Mickey Dees, wouldn't you?" Parker pushed forward again and buried his face in her hair.

Tamsen was quiet for a minute. Then she said, "When you come home, are you going to talk loud?"

Mama hugged Parker close to her body. "No, Tamsen. Never again. I'm not going to talk loud, and I'm not going to throw dishes, and I'm not going to …"

Mama hesitated and then stood and pulled Parker up with her. She set him in a chair and put one of the boxes of fries in front of him. She laid out a sandwich, opened and flattened the paper, pulled the top off the burger, and put it to one side on the paper. She put the pickles in a pile and then moved burger off the bottom bun and put the bottom bun on the other side. "Just the way you like it," she said to Parker and put her hand on his head. With both hands, Parker reached for the pile of pickles and stuffed them into his mouth and chewed. Mama stroked the top of Parker's head and then fished in the bag and pulled out a straw. She bit off the end of the paper and, using her fingertips, peeled off the sleeve. She stuck it into one of the cups with a scraping sound and set it next to Parker. The drink was orange soda, Tamsen could see, Parker's favorite.

Mama pulled a long French fry from Parker's pile and stepped closer to Tamsen. She crouched down and extended her hand toward Tamsen, holding the French fry in her palm.

"Would you …" Mama said.

Tamsen looked at Mama and then slowly reached for the French fry, all the while keeping her eyes on Mama's face. Using just her fingertips, she plucked the fry from Mama's palm. As she started to pull back, Mama clutched Tamsen's hand with both of hers and brought it back toward her body. Tamsen was jerked forward. Tamsen turned her head and focused on Parker, who had finished the pickles and started on the French fries.

"Look at me," Mama said. "Look at me?"

Tamsen wanted to, but she couldn't.

Hard Men

For the hard men who want love but know that it won't come. – "Shake the Dust," Anis Mojgani

J OHNNY GOOD SHOT AND KILLED HIS CRANKED-OUT FATHER. The tinny smell of the three shots overwhelmed his father's chemical odor and the smell of bacon from the breakfast Johnny had made, hoping he could get his father to eat, to stop the obsessing, fidgeting, floor-creaking rounds down the trailer house corridor and back while picking at the sores around his thin-lipped grimace.

The way his father had died was not like on TV, one shot and then keeled over, not moving. No. Though Johnny had been aiming the pistol for his father's heart—his father's left but his right, next the sternum, above the xyphoid process—his adrenalin and shaking hands made him shoot low the first time and hit his father's belly. He could tell because that's where the blood began to seep into the once-white cotton undershirt. His father had looked at him, hands spread in surprise, but then bent his head to the side like he had believed his son would do it all along, like he did when Johnny used to creep out of bed and into his parents' bedroom after lights-out to ask his father a manufactured question to put off sleep a little longer, just so he wouldn't have to be in his room alone. Johnny imagined him doing that exact head-tip to his high school students when they missed the question, *On the periodical table of elements, what does Gd stand for?* This was something Johnny hadn't actually seen because he wasn't a junior till next year and so hadn't taken his father's chemistry class.

After that first shot, his father came after him, hands bared and grasping, so Johnny took a deep breath as adrenalin coursed through him and clenched his hands tightly around the pistol grip to quell the shaking and aimed again and then fired two shots in quick succession. One, at least, hit the target because blood splashed across the microwave and the counter, and then his father went down, first on one knee and then onto his back, and blood gushed out from underneath like water from a hose. The carpet resisted at first, and the blood ran down the sloping floor and pooled under the couch, but then the scotch-guarded fibers gave in and the liquid began to soak and seep. There was so much blood, more blood than Johnny thought possible. His father hadn't just laid there, though, even as he was bleeding out. He kept trying to get up, his sharp-boned body slopping in the red sticky liquid, his rotted teeth bared, his focus pulling back from Johnny to the middle distance. His attempts got weaker and weaker until he lay there staring upwards, and then he wasn't staring, though his eyes were open.

Johnny knew that his father would kill him. His father had killed the pizza delivery guy the night before with Johnny's baseball bat. His father had used the baseball bat because he'd left the shotgun in the living room and his pistol out in the truck. Johnny had known the pizza delivery guy a little. His name was Don, short for Donavan. A few years older and already graduated. A good first baseman when they were kids. Lived with his mom in one of those apartments above the stores in Old Town. Tall, skinny, and pimply but with a sense of humor. One time, the guy had lent him a pair of socks for gym class. Now, Johnny knew that he shouldn't have asked anyone to come anywhere near the house, especially for something as stupid as pizza, and he certainly shouldn't have invited the guy in. He should've heeded the signs, that feeling that shit would happen soon, bad shit. What had he been thinking? Don had smiled at him at the door and said, "Johnny, man, you look like crap." Which had prompted Johnny to go look for another dollar to tip, which prompted him to invite Don in to wait, which prompted his father to launch from the back of the trailer, bat held high over his head, screaming "Fucking agents of change!"

It helped that this man his father had become was not at all like the father from before. His father used to wear short-sleeved plaid western shirts in off colors with black and navy blue ties and dress pants. He used to shine his brown leather shoes with a horse-bristle brush, *ka-shshsh*, *ka-shshsh*, every Sunday night while watching the news. His body used to sag and paunch from his love of butter brickle ice cream and potatoes fried in bacon grease and drowned in ketchup. This was the father who had insisted Johnny and his little brother Mark, whom everyone called Newt, be at the breakfast table promptly at 6:45 to eat the sausage and eggs or blueberry pancakes their mother had cooked. The father who hugged them goodbye when they were little, and then when they were older he ruffled their hair or put his hand on their shoulders before he walked out the door in the morning. Homework right after dinner and before TV, no exceptions. "Five minutes with Darwin is worth five months sitting with a sitcom," he said, his brow beetled with sincerity.

But now, his father was no longer a person but a thing, lying on the floor with its horrid red shadow. The essential element of life had precipitated, evaporated, something. It was there, and now it was gone, and Johnny had seen it disappear. Johnny felt the urge to try to capture it and put it back. What could he use? A blanket, a butterfly net, a turkey roasting pan? He knew it was illogical just as he glanced around the room for something, anything, to contain it.

And then guilt made Johnny's body weaken and twinge. Johnny hadn't saved him. Up until that very last moment, until he saw the look in his father's eyes, Johnny had believed that it was possible to pull him out of the clutches of this thing that had taken him over. Had he really believed? Well, maybe he had needed to believe. Maybe not belief but hope against all the odds, against the empirical evidence. All he needed to do was separate this thing, this monster, this demon-possession, from the physical body that was his father. His father was still in there. He was. Johnny had seen him, less just recently, but still there in the small gestures—a certain way of sitting on the couch leaning forward, one shoulder propped higher than the other. The habit of softly closing the door and pushing it until it latched with an audible click when he went to the bathroom. Hooking his keys held with two fingers onto the house-shaped brass key holder on the wall next to the door. When they had lived in the house, the hooks had been attached to a wooden mail organizer.

Guilt was quickly replaced by anger. First at his father— but it was all too fresh and there was his father and he couldn't be angry with his father, only this thing that had overtaken him, and, anyway, anger at his father would bring him to his knees later, much much later. Now, quickly, the anger turned inward. Had he been paying attention, he could've sensed it as it shot out of him toward his father and then boomeranged in a wide circle and zeroed in and pierced him cleanly. He should've been more prepared, he should've thought things through, this could've been prevented, it was all his fault. There should've been something he could've done, or not done.

He shouldn't've invited Don in—that was for sure. He shouldn't've borrowed the little .38 from his friend Benji, even if those deliberate and soft-spoken guys his father had been hanging out with kept coming around. His choice to stay with his father instead of moving to California with his mother and Newt—would that have made a difference? Would his father still have ended up dead if he'd ran away with his mother instead of staying to try to save his father? He glanced at his father's body. It looked like that of a starved and beaten dog— pale skin stretched drum-tight over knobs of bones, oozing sores, lips pulled back to show blackish teeth. Yes. His father would've died. No doubt about it. Johnny's presence in the house neither held him back nor pushed him toward the drug. Johnny's presence had long been irrelevant.

Now, what to do now? Shifting the pistol to his left hand, Johnny tilted it until he found the safety and with his index finger pressed it on. He stepped over the river of blood and to the couch, set the pistol on an open *Sports Illustrated*, picked the shotgun up off the cushions, and propped it in the corner made by the couch and the wall. He sat down to think, his knees on his elbows and his chin on the heels of his hands.

It had always been his father and him, really. Every family had favorites, sure, but in their case, it was no secret and there had been no apologies. It had been Dad and Johnny and then Mom and Newt. Johnny played baseball and their father came to the games. Newt's work placed in the art show and their mother attended. Johnny sat on the couch watching basketball with their father, while Newt helped their mother in the kitchen. It was as if their parents were at opposite poles with Johnny and Newt stretched between them, the only thing holding them together. And then not holding them together. There were times that their father was almost enough for Johnny, but then there were other times. He didn't think to blame his mother, only Newt, and so he and Newt weren't close. Johnny was also sure that Newt was gay, although the last time Johnny had seen Newt, age 12, seven months ago, Newt was just starting to realize it. Over the course of a year, Newt had become secretive and introverted. Johnny felt bad for all the shit he was going to have to go through, although Johnny had done nothing at school to stop it or to make his brother feel better.

The smell from the bathroom, even with the door and the outside window shut and duct-taped, was getting stronger. It was a smell that Johnny would repress until, years later, he would drive windows open by a country trash dump with the ballooning carcasses of dead livestock. The memory of sitting on that stiff couch in the trailer staring at the body of his father surrounded by the stench of the decomposing lye-soaked body of Donovan in the bathtub will force him to stomp on the brakes and wrench open the door and lean out just in time to spew green-yellow bile onto the gravel. But in the present, there is too much of the shadow of adrenalin in his system for his body to give in.

Action. He should be figuring out what to do. He needs to do something. The fact is that he has shot his own father, a once-respected teacher and coach—probably still respected by former students who had moved away and their parents who remembered his knack for communicating the intricacies of valence and chemical structure and his firm but inspiring presence on the basketball court. But Johnny couldn't think about that now. Not with the man he loved (once loved?) lying before him. In that moment, Johnny was overtaken with tenderness. Daddy tickling his ribs and squeezing his knee as Johnny screamed, "No, Daddy," in a way that meant, "Yes, Daddy." Daddy swaying his hips back and forth as he dribbled the ball and gently taunted his son on the concrete pad he had poured on the property of their old house just for that purpose. The story of his father being denied his dream of becoming a nuclear physicist by a small and small-minded college professor. At the thought, Johnny cried fat and sloppy tears. At 15, he had not yet mastered the art of transmuting his pain, not into sorrow but into rage. That would come later, in prison and in a series of menial low-paying jobs. His eyes bathing his face and his shoulders shuddering, he became the 15-year-old boy he was.

And then he wanted to call his mom. No. He didn't want to call her. He wanted her here sitting next to him, her arms wrapped around him like she so often did with Newt, both a gesture of bringing him into her and of excluding the world, Johnny, and his father. What did he want? He wanted to feel safe—that it was the world that those arms suggested, not the world he had started to realize it was. He rubbed the snot dripping from the tip of his nose onto the shoulder of his shirt in a quick and fierce gesture and then fished his cell phone out of the pocket of his jeans. He flipped it open and pushed and held the number four. Yes, he had programmed her number into his speed dial, but this would be the first time he actually dialed it. Number four was the number of people in their family but also the number he had guessed in a game to see whether he or Newt got to go to the grocery store with their mother one Sunday. He had no doubt that had his father not been standing there his mother would have taken Newt and that would've been that, but instead it became a game, something his father was fond of, and so held the true number in his mind, because his father would not cheat, and it was Johnny instead of Newt who got to go. And then his mother, for a reason Johnny never knew and never understood, stopped for a flavored ice at the stand in the park and sat on the benches in the shade of the cottonwoods to eat it. Johnny sucked on the straw of his sour apple ice and ignored the siren song of the slide and swings and the kids screaming to sit quietly next to his mother and feel the warmth of her shoulder next to his ear. From then on, he considered the number four not their family's but his and hers exclusively, and even though he had never called it, he often flipped open his phone and touched it gently with the pad of his index finger, especially on those nights when his father's friends were over and he sat in his bedroom ignoring his homework and watching the empty chair that he had propped under his doorknob.

But now he pressed and held the button and it rang once, twice, three times, a fourth, and then someone picked up. "Hello?" It was his mother's voice, but in it was all the distance between Wyoming and California, all the distance that had always been in their lives. Had she looked at the caller ID and seen his name and still her voice sounded like this? He couldn't breathe, much less talk. No air came in and he couldn't force any air out. She said again, "Hello?" This time her voice was quieter, an extended echo of itself, like her mind had moved on and wasn't even in the thing she was saying. It had moved on to what she would be doing in thirty seconds or that afternoon or on the weekend. Perhaps she would be making corn-flake pork chops for supper? Maybe they were going to that café on the beach to play sand volleyball? Her mind had skittered past the existence of whomever was on the other end of the call. Johnny couldn't take it anymore. He flipped the phone closed, tossed it onto the couch next to him, and laid back against the cushions with such force that the couch thumped against the wall.

After the months of gathering evidence, Johnny will be tried as an adult for double murder and sentenced 25 to life in a maximum security prison. While in prison, he will learn that the world is as hard a place as he suspected. He will not be able to go to his father's funeral, of course, and he won't be able to go to his mother's funeral (breast cancer) nor his brother's funeral (AIDS). He will be released on parole after 22 years on good behavior. Once he is out, he'll find the world a confusing and unstructured place. He will never marry because he cannot bring himself to trust anyone to live in the same space he does. And of course he will die alone, like we all do. But he doesn't know this, sitting here on the couch. In his mind, he is not a criminal, a person flawed and innately dangerous. That will come later. Sitting on the couch, he is a sophomore in high school, a member of the honor society who likes to play baseball and hang out with friends in the gym at the rec center, who has his eye on a girl who likes to wear purple capri pants and whose thin shoulders are striped with multiple pigtails, who looks forward to someday maybe being a teacher like his old man because it seems like a cool thing to do. Even these last couple of months has not taken that away.

It remained for him to decide what to do. The most logical thing was to run. Was it really his fault? Any one of the guys who stopped by the house could've done it. The cops had arrested his father enough times to know about that. And Donovan decomposing in the bathtub—it was logical that Johnny's father had at least arranged it, as he was the one who knew about chemistry and that industrial-grade lye stolen from the high school AP lab would do the trick. Would they think that his father had killed Don? The baseball bat had been tossed into an open field, so no fingerprints or blood to point one direction or another. He could wipe down the gun and walk out the door, shutting it behind him so hopefully no one would smell anything for days, giving him a head start. He'd take the bike because they'd trace a car and the money his father had in his wallet for his next buy and some food and water. It would just take a couple of days to bike to the cabin he'd once gone to with Benji, an old broken down thing way off the beaten path.

He'd stay till he ran out of food. That would give him time to figure things out.

What was he thinking? This wasn't a cop show. He had killed his father, and if there was one thing his father had taught him, it was that there were no shortcuts. It didn't matter if you tried to get out of things, to find a way to skirt your duties—you would face the consequences. If you stole candy at in the grocery line, it didn't matter if you quickly stuffed it into your mouth. You had to tell the manager and then work there after school every Tuesday for a month to learn the value of what you had stolen. If you didn't study for the algebra test, your grade would reflect your efforts. But if you did what was right—put in the time on the court practicing your jump shot or in the library reading the history of the Trojan War—the world was such a place that you would be rewarded. No. Better to stand up and take it, to face the problem head on and take the punishment as a man would. It didn't matter what his father was now—what mattered was what he had been and what he had taught Johnny to be.

His eyes wide in their innocence, Johnny picked up his cell phone, flipped it open, and dialed 911.

Nose to the Fence

I T WAS EARLY SUMMER, and profligate clumps of willow and aspen hugged the stream meander. Beyond, gentle hills skirted upwardly toothing mountains, slate blue and ethereal. The sinking sun brought Cindy relief from the afternoon's pressing heat. The claustrophobic odor of baking dirt gave way to the pungent wet scents of peppermint and wild onions, and cool air pocketed the creek bottom near the stream. "Cindy, you see to those boys, see that they don't get lost," her step-dad Bud said as he rode by on Dirty. He tipped his head toward the three dudes from New York— *guests*, Cindy reminded herself, don't call them *dudes*. Cindy sat on Twister and made sure she didn't roll her eyes.

Some people laughed when Cindy told them about the family dude ranch. "You mean people *pay you money* to work it?" they'd say, but it wasn't like that. Even the people who already knew how to ride took some babysitting. They'd ride off by themselves and get lost or demand special food or get sick at the altitude. Above all, try as they might they weren't much actual help. She had to herd dudes just like she herded cows, and the cows were easier.

These three boys from New York were teenagers, a couple years older than Cindy though they acted younger. Careless, with no sense of responsibility. Earlier, the youngest of the three had let his horse wander into the middle of the herd, which parted like the Red Sea. Frustrated, Cindy yelled, "Hey!" When the guy noticed where he was, he stopped his horse dead in its tracks. The herd slid around him like a school of tuna. When the herd's tail end caught up, the two other guys had rode up beside him and started razzing him: "*Whoa up, there, cowboy*," they said, "thought you were a cow there for a minute," and "Thought I was going to have to *ride you out of the herd.*" Their voices emphasized the western phrases like they were bit players in *City Slicker*.

"Yes, sir," she said to Bud and nodded. She, Bud, her older brother Jake, and her cousin Wyatt always spread out among the dudes—someone leading the way, a couple in the middle entertaining, and one taking up the lag end and chatting with the stragglers—but Bud was only having her do it because he didn't want to deal with the young guys. Bud was an ex-teacher, and Cindy always imagined he'd been one of those teachers who liked to get under the skin of the guys in his class.

HER REAL DAD, BIG-BELLIED AND USUALLY SO QUIETLY MEASURED, had left when Cindy was ten. He hadn't said why, just one day drove to town for parts and ran off and left them. She'd been on her way in from the fields, and he'd driven past but not seen her there in the pasture. She'd seen him, though, facing forward, eyes intent on the road ahead. The look on his face stuck with her. Cindy had searched her memory of that day for some indication of his aim, but there had been none, and it soon blended with other memories of him, so that her every recall was tainted, heavy with ironic foreboding. She was sure that she had caused it somehow yet equally sure that she meant so little to him that he shrugged her off and tossed her and the whole family aside like a disposable calving glove. She later found out that he'd run off with this girl just out of high school named Jesse Bell. The girl had long dark-brown hair that swung to her waist and what the fashion magazines called an hour-glass figure.

Then Mom had married Bud, an out-of-work teacher from Last Chance who moved onto the ranch and took over the running of things. Bud was very different from her father. Instead of a slow and easy-going nature, Bud brought a teacher's love of order and correction. Things needed to be just so. Mom kept the house cleaner and cooked more elaborate meals. In addition to school, homework, feeding chickens and gathering their eggs, slopping the fattening hogs, tending cattle, training horses, and all their regular duties, Cindy and Jake spent the little time left cutting weeds in places they never went and mending fences that were never used and reading things they weren't interested in. These efforts almost never lived up to expectation. The ranch wasn't doing well—never had been, really, even when their dad was around—so they started taking on dudes to make ends meet, advertising themselves as a real working cattle ranch who liked to have visitors. And so there were even more jobs that needed done, appearances were even more important, and Bud's critical eye and sharp tongue had all the more reason to lash out. However, he was also aware that outsiders cast a jaundiced eye on cussing out your kids, so his tirades were more subtle.

Cindy pulled back on the reins, and Twister stopped but sidestepped as others ambled by. He wanted to follow them.

Twister was the size of a large pony but had the slim build and delicate head of a horse. He was a black and white paint—like a Guernsey cow, his body was an archipelago of expansive black and white peninsulas and islands. He was the first horse she'd broken from scratch. They'd had her work him because the guys who usually broke the horses were too heavy, while she was only fourteen and just a bit of thing.

In among the guests, her brother Jake rode by and tipped his cowboy hat and made sucking motions with his lips. He meant, *sucking the hind titty again*. Then he gave her the toothy smile that made Cindy glad she was his sister. She smiled back.

She waited until the three guys rode past. They talked with each other and hardly glanced her direction, and she turned to follow them. They kept their slow pace, their tired horses happy to oblige. She decided to ride behind them the whole way home, no matter what Bud would say later. She watched their backs as they rode. They were all short and stocky with dark hair—one with a pudgy body and black curls and the other two obviously brothers with stocky bodies and brown straight hair. They looked about the age of Jake—seniors in high school, maybe—only they acted younger, razzing each other and not paying attention. The pudgy boneless one slumped in the saddle and joked incessantly. Cindy made a mental note to check Sundance, his horse, for saddle sores and maybe put on an extra pad. The soft-spoken elder of the two brothers had a milky complexion and cheeks that blushed from his cheekbones to his chin. Cindy wondered whether it caused him grief at school. The younger brother was a slenderer version of the older, and he sat straight but loose in the saddle, as if he were comfortable there. She wondered whether he'd ridden before. It certainly looked that way, but where would a person find a horse in a place like New York City?

The pudgy guy pulled to a stop and the brothers stopped too, and so did Cindy. Then, with the grace of an elephant seal, he swung off Sundance and dropped his reins to the ground— something Cindy never did unless she wanted to walk home— and started rummaging in the saddle bags. He pulled out a granola bar and said, "At least I'm getting my roughage. Gran'll be so happy." The other two laughed. He ate the granola bar in two big bites, tossed the wrapper on the ground, wiped his fingers on his chinos, and then tried to remount. He left the reins hanging from Sundance's chin while he grabbed the left-hand stirrup and tried to swing his right leg up to his belly and stick his boot into the opening. Cindy said nothing— he'd figure out what he was doing wrong once he tried to swing over. After much hopping and patience on Sundance's part, he succeeded in getting his right foot into the stirrup. Then he grabbed the stirrup leathers with both hands and pulled. He pulled himself to standing in the stirrups and then it came to him what he had done: if he swung over, his left leg would swing over the horse's withers and he would face backwards. With a *fwump*, he let himself down to the ground. The brothers laughed again.

"Boarding school paying off," the younger one said.

"I'm such a idjet," the pudgy guy said. Then he glanced at Cindy and frowned.

Cindy realized she was just sitting there doing nothing— that was what prompted his glance—so she said, "I'm sorry.

Would you like some help?" and swung down off Twister and walked up to him.

"A little help would be nice," the guy said.

"I'm sorry. I should've helped before."

The guy raised his eyebrows.

"Here," Cindy said. "No big deal. Wyatt once swung all the way on before he realized. He was a city kid too once. I'm Cindy, by the way." She held out her hand.

The pudgy guy hesitated and then took it. "Eddy. Eddy Silver." He nodded toward the other two. "Jonathan and David Greene."

Jonathan, the older brother, nodded and smiled at her. The younger brother David also had a smile on his lips, but his eyes were different. Jonathan's crinkled at the corners, while David's were wide and focused and didn't blink. Even from where she stood, she could see that they were green as a tropical sea. At first Cindy didn't look away because his eyes felt magnetized, but then she didn't look away because it was like he was egging her on, pushing her. His eyebrows raised but still he didn't blink. If that's the way he's going to be, she thought—she stared right back at him. It went on and on. Finally, he smiled and looked away. Later that year while reading a romance novel, Cindy would come across the words, "and then their smoldering eyes locked." That's what had happened, she guessed, but it hadn't felt the way the book made it sound, with headstrong heroines and tall, dark, and handsome men ravished and ravishing. It felt more like on the playground when the Stewart boy came up and pushed her down and then Jake told her she had to go over and push him down or the kid would do it again. She hadn't, and the kid had laughed at her with the other boys, so she went over and punched him instead.

JUST LIKE JAKE TO GUIDE HER—he had always been good to her. He gave her sound advice, and she could trust him, like when she broke Twister. She'd been scared shitless. That first day, her hands shook so badly she'd dropped the halter. Early that spring in the home place's round corral out back of the dilapidated barn, she started him. Their breath—hers and Jake's and Twister's—billowed in white clouds, and the ground frost that lined the shadows of the fence rail narrowed and then pinched out in the slow slip of the morning sun. Jake with his blonde halo of hair stood in the center of the corral, shoulders relaxed, the turns of rope in his left hand and the loop in his right. Twister stood broadside to them, body pressed flat against the wooden rails. Legs quivering, he lifted his muzzle and focused on them with one wild eye, more white than dark.

"You got to relax," Jake said to Cindy. "If you're scared and he's scared, all hell'll break lose."

Cindy did not reply. She didn't want to let on how weak she felt, how her bowels rumbled and threatened to cut lose. But of course Jake could tell. He was ~~after~~ all her beloved brother, the soother of nightmares, the playground defender, the bandager of wounds.

"You got to be the one in control," Jake said, his face turned to her, his body toward the horse. "Gentle but firm. You got to let him know you're in charge and get him to trust that and to trust you."

Cindy nodded obediently, sharply, once, then again.

81

Jake turned back to Twister. He took a step toward the horse and began twirling his rope over his head. Twister bolted around the corral and slowed to a trot on the other side, glancing at them but then nosing his way along the fence, looking for a crack, a way out. He snorted and turned, whirling on his hindquarters.

Cindy wanted to tell Jake to stop, to let it go—couldn't he see the horse's terror? She'd do it herself, but softer, more gently. She'd give the horse breathing room, give him time. Couldn't Jake see he needed that? She glanced to Jake. Jake was kind and good with horses, and the mounts he broke were invariably the most responsive, the most content—if that were a qualification for a horse. Torn, she glanced between them, man and animal. It must be done, if the horse was to be tamed, but why did it sometimes seem that life was filled with those things that were the most terrifying, the most painful?

Jake swung his rope for a time, keeping the same amount of distance between himself and Twister, getting him used to the movement. When the horse ran away, Jake followed. When the horse had calmed somewhat, he twirled the loop twice above his head and tossed it with soft ease over Twister's neck. When Jake pulled the loop taut, Twister reared in panic and crashed over sideways with a *whump*. He lay for a second breathing heavily before bracing his front hooves and bobbing his head to lever himself to his feet. Then he stood sideways to them and pulled, resisting the rope. Jake braced the rope over his hip and leaned into it, applying more pressure. Twister fought, panic shivering through him, but the minute he turned to face them, Jake loosed the slack and gave him his breath. Twister seemed confused, shaking his head, but his ears were forward, which meant he was listening. Talking over his shoulder, Jake said, "You've got to apply pressure just as long as he's not doing what you want. The minute he does do it, release the pressure, give him relief. He'll learn that doing what you ask is easier. He'll learn to trust you." Jake soon turned the rope over to Cindy, and she worked the horse for the rest of the morning. She wasn't sure who was shaking worse, her or Twister, but by the end of it, she could pat him on gently on the muzzle.

Later that day, after Cindy had grained Twister and turned him out to pasture, she had wondered if that was the way life was, the way God was, if He existed. What were the lessons she was supposed to be learning? If that was so, she was ready for the release to come, the indication she was heading in the right direction. When was that going to happen? Her dad leaving—what was the lesson in all that, Cindy wondered, the thing God was trying to teach her? Before that, everything was stable and level, built on solid ground, but ever since then, everything seemed to come at Cindy from the side, pressing in on her, pushing her off-kilter. Some part of the bedrock upon which their lives rested had been blasted away, and the world hung precariously upon the rimrocks.

CINDY HELPED EDDY MOUNT. She showed him how to gather up the reins, put his foot in the stirrup, grab the saddle horn and saddle back, and swing up and over. "Push with your legs and pull with your arms and you'll get there slicker than a greased snake," she said. Once Eddy was in the saddle, they started walking again, and this time Cindy walked with them. She rode between Jonathan and David, with Eddy on the other side of Jonathan. As they talked, she kept an eye on Billy Bud,

David's palomino, because he didn't like Twister and had a tendency to bite. But Billie Bud was tired and only laid his ears back a little.

"So, you go to school?" Jonathan said.

"Yep," Cindy said. "Over in Last Chance. It's about an hour bus ride. Or Jake drives. Drove. He graduated."

"What do you study there?" David said. *"Readin', writin',* and *'rithmetic?"* His voice took on that same singsong quality as when he mentioned ranch terms.

Ignoring his tone, Cindy said, "Last year we read James Welch and Willa Cather and Ernest Hemingway. And we did some pre-calc algebra."

"Really," David said. "So, you know what *ain't* really means?"

Cindy tilted her head down, raised her eyebrows, and looked at him. She took a deliberate breath and then said, *"Ain't* is a contraction of *am not* and so should only be used with *I.* Used correctly anyhow." Bud's training paying off—'bout time, she thought.

"How old *are* you?" David said.

Jonathan quickly intervened, "Eddy and I graduated from Whitworth last semester, and David's just a junior." He must be the peacemaker in the family, like Jake, Cindy thought.

"Old enough to beat you at cards," Cindy said to David. She didn't really play cards, but it was a saying and she didn't want to tell them she was only fourteen.

"Yeah?" David said. "Seven card stud, aces wild."

"David," Jonathan said.

"Yeah, *David,"* Eddy said.

Cindy hesitated and then said, "Don't have any cards on me, but I bet I could beat you arm wrestling." She wasn't sure she could, but David looked soft, and she had lifted bales all winter and saddles all summer. She never beat Jake nor Wyatt, as they were older and worked just as hard as she, but she'd beaten a cocky kid at school when she was younger. Not something she did a lot, but she knew she was strong for a girl.

"Kay," David said. "There, on that rock." The gray and pink granite rock he pointed to jutted from the ground like a narrow island and was the right height for kneeling. It was not a separate boulder—it was bedrock that had outlasted its neighbors through eons of battering wind and water, an island above the ground that was supported by a sculptured pedestal connected to bedrock toward one end. Cindy had once stood on that rock to mount bareback on a retired racehorse named Too Tall.

"All right," Cindy said.

Eddy looked at David and said, "All right, I'll bet your iPod she beats you, girley-man."

"Easy money," David said.

They all dismounted. Cindy handed her reins to Jonathan, who smiled and nodded with what looked like encouragement.

Cindy knelt on one side, extended her arm, and placed her elbow on the rough surface. She held her hand open and relaxed. She could feel a rock poke her knee, so she shifted and pushed it out of the way and then lowered her butt a little so she felt centered. Then she looked up at David.

David was standing with his head to one side, looking at the rock. He said, "You got the higher side, but you're a girl, so you can have it."

85

Cindy pushed herself up and said, "No way." She walked around the rock to the other side and kneeled.

Eddy, who stood back holding his chin with his right hand, his elbow propped on his other arm, said, "Legally, Cindy, you laid claim to your territory first, and even if you didn't mean to, you got the advantage. Jonathan?"

"I agree," Jonathan said. "David, you have no grounds for appeal if she beats your ass."

Cindy cocked her head and wrinkled her forehead and looked at David. David shrugged, so Cindy returned to the other side of the rock, knelt down, and put her elbow back down. With his fingertips, David hiked up his pants legs, stepping from one foot to the other as he did so, and then squatted on the other side. When his body was this close, Cindy could smell his aftershave. It was Polo, same as Bud wore when he took Cindy's mom out dancing. It was too strong, and Cindy tried not to wrinkle her nose. Why would anyone put on perfume out here? She had no idea. She decided not to look in his eyes and so instead she focused on his hands. Even though David was short, his hands were big, and when he reached out and gripped her palm, her hand disappeared. His forearm was longer than hers, something that the higher platform on her side did not quite compensate for, so he had that advantage. He stutter-gripped, trying to get a better hold, but he did not squeeze hard, so Cindy squeezed more tightly. He loosened his grip even more. She shook his hand back and forth, making his wrist flop, and then looked at his face. It was blank, no trace of either a smirk nor concern. He was not taking this seriously. She determined she would make him take her seriously, see past whatever preconceived notions he held.

86

"All right," Eddy said. "I'll say, one, two, three, go, and then you go. Cindy?"

"Yep," Cindy said.

"David?" Eddy said.

"I'm ready," David said.

"One, two, three, *go!*"

Not sure what strategy to take, Cindy decided to go for it, to give it her all because she wasn't sure how long she could last. If David got her wrist over or held out for a while, she wouldn't be able to manage. So when Eddy said go, she bore down for all she was worth. She grunted as she turned her body into it, locking her wrist and elbow. She didn't meet much resistance at first. After holding steady for a split second, she pushed his hand down some, and then down some more, first an eighty-degree angle, then a forty-five, then a thirty. She didn't look at him. Instead, she focused on her arm.

"You're strong," David said. "Shit. You're strong."

Cindy risked a glance at his face, which was scrunched up around the forehead. David started pressing back. He squeezed, and Cindy felt the bones in the back of her hand grate together. She made sure she did not wince. Their hands shook from his effort to push back up, but the thirty degrees held, and held, and held. Cindy's breath started coming faster as her body ran out of oxygen. She could feel the muscles in her upper arms tiring, and she knew she didn't have long. She gritted her teeth and bent her head and pushed for all she was worth. She made a *hmmm* sound low under her breath. Her arm started burning, and she thought she felt something give way near her wrist, but it didn't hurt so she kept on. She glanced up at David's face again. His brow was smooth now and his black eyebrows made an inverted half-moon on his forehead. For the first time since they'd met, his face had opened up. It was like he was looking at her and really seeing her. Then he glanced down at their hands. It wasn't an avoidance of her eyes. It was slow and deliberate. It was him asking, *do you want me to let it go, to relax, to let you win? If you want me to, I will.* The look wasn't arrogance, and it wasn't pity. It was like she'd earned it. With a small quick jerk, she shook her head *no*. He looked at her again and then, very slowly, tipped his forehead down and then up like he was bowing. Then he started pushing again. Even though Cindy pushed for all she was worth, their hands angled up, slowly at first, forty-five degrees, fifty, eighty. Then he had her. At a little over ninety degrees, her wrist gave way and her arm collapsed.

He held her hand down for a split second and then released it slowly. She pulled hers back. It was numb, so she opened and closed it, trying to get her circulation back. Then she noticed the back of her hand was scraped white and flecked with blood where it had made contact with the granite. She covered it up with her other hand.

"You almost lost it, Davie," Eddy said. "She almost had you."

David didn't say anything. Out of the corner of her eye, she could see him watching her, but she refused to meet his eyes. She kept her head down as she stood up. He stood up too and then bent over and dipped his head like he was trying to hook her gaze, but she turned her head away. Jonathan and Eddy glanced at each other and without saying anything turned to mount their horses. As she turned to walk to her horse, David skipped around in front of her and stopped, forcing her to stop.

She turned to walk around him but he took a step sideways to block her path. Finally, jaw clenched and eyebrows raised, she looked him in the face. Again, his eyebrows made a half-moon, and he mouthed the word *sorry*. Cindy hesitated and then shrugged. David smiled, genuine this time, and stepped out of her path. They both walked to their horses and mounted.

As they again started for home, Cindy's and David's horses fell in beside each other, with Eddy and Jonathan up ahead.

"I've never met anyone like you," David said, his voice shed of its mocking tone. "Smart but not afraid to show it."

"Yeah?" Smart? Was she?

"Yeah. The girls in the City are JAPs."

"What?" They were Japanese?

"Jewish American Princesses," he explained. "You know, think they're royalty. You have to treat them like glass."

"Aren't they smart?" She couldn't imagine girls were that different, even if they were raised in a city.

David snorted. "I guess. But they don't act that way. It's like they're ashamed of any brains they do have." He glanced at her. "And they'd never do what you did. Arm wrestle."

"Well, we arm wrestle." Cindy didn't know whether to be proud or ashamed, and she felt a mixture of both. "Anyway, it doesn't matter if I am smart. I could be—I don't know—Einstein, and nobody'd notice."

"Maybe you should beat them up," David said with a smile in his voice.

Cindy smiled too.

"Or you could move East," he said. "What do you think? Become a *New Yawker*?" His voice contained vast affection, even as it was slightly mocking.

Would she ever love a place that much? She reached out with her senses to consider the question. The light had faded, and it was almost pitch dark. They moved through the pockets of heat and coolness without guiding their horses, trusting them to place their own feet and carry them home. The shapes of hills to the west were backlit by the remaining twilight, and a light trace of the trail shown faintly on the ground. In the distance, a grouse drummed its chest, slowly at first but ending in a quick *thump-thump-thump*. She heard the yip of a coyote, sure to be followed by its packmates. Yes, another yip and then a quick rising yowl. She could smell plants growing in the marshland in the next draw and the strong odor of the surrounding sagebrush. The breeze had died down and the air was still but fresh with the rising of the night air. Did she love this place? She wasn't sure, but as she thought about it, she didn't think so. It wasn't love, or what she understood to be love as others described it: an uncomplicated positive emotion, direct attraction, you just knew it. Her emotions about the ranch were anything but uncomplicated, and she didn't know if she would ever understand them, nor be free of them. It was as if the red ochre of the place had, over the years, simply sifted painfully into her bones. Now, the idea of another place—New York, say—blew through her and opened her up. The idea that she would not always be in this place, that it would not simply close over her one day, had never before occurred to her. Could she move? Really? Could she? It seemed such an impossible thing, yet now that the idea had been formed with his words, it sunk deep within her.

Then it came to her: had this been what her father had felt? He had grown up on a neighboring ranch and spent his whole life here. Had the girl Jesse been his breath of fresh air, his second chance at living, at relieving the pressure? Cindy took a deep breath. The thought lifted a burden from her that she had not known she carried, and for the first time since he had left she felt a softness toward him, sorrow even. She took another deep breath and held it in for as long as she could and then released it slowly.

It was full-on dark with a half-moon rising over the mountains as they reined up to the corral at the home place. They dismounted, she took the reins from David, and then after some hesitation he went up to the house for supper, saying "You're not coming?"

"I'll join in later," she said. This, whatever it was, could wait.

Cindy watched his form meld with the darkness. A night bird made a *twee-twee*, *twee-twee* as it rose into the sky. Cindy took off her hat, and the breeze felt cool through her sweaty hair. She led Twister and Tonto, David's horse, into the corral and closed the gate. As she led them through into the bigger corral with all the other horses, she could smell their sweat and the pleasant odor of their shit. She heard one on the far side of the corral rolling in the dust—*whump, whump*. Then, one by one, she led the horses that were still saddled into the barn, unsaddled them, and tied them each into a stall. She retrieved a five-gallon bucket of oats from the barrel and then dipped the dented coffee can's worth into each feed bin, saving Twister

91

for last. She talked low as she walked around behind him, making sure he knew she was there. She sidled up next to him and dumped the oats into his bin. He extended his nose and sniffed her, and she felt his warm moist breath and tickling muzzle hairs on her arm. Then he turned and delicately nibbled at the oats. Cindy walked back to the open barn door and leaned against the rough wood of the frame in a slanting beam of moonlight. The world was a gentle place filled with munching.

Control Erosion

I T WAS CATASTROPHIC FAILURE NORMAN WAS WORRIED ABOUT. The bridge was being undermined. The river meandered to the left where it came from under the bridge's pylons, and over time the water had seriously undercut the rock riprap that protected the right bank and the bridge itself. It was Baer's Law—because of the forces of the earth's rotation, in the northern hemisphere the right banks of rivers were hardest hit by erosion.

Norman saw everything as a series of forces to be measured, calculated, and—where possible—controlled. Take, for example, the bridge. Gravity exerted a certain predictable downward force on the elements of the bridge, while the ground exerted an equal and opposite force upwards, thus maintaining equilibrium. Cars and trucks exerted vectored loads on the bridge's expanse. Wind exerted a certain amount of force, but on a fairly short beam bridge such as this one, it was negligible. Finally, water exerted a persistent force against everything on the ground—the sand and soil, the rocks, the pylons, the creek banks. The attenuation structure—the rock riprap with its geosynthetic fabric liner—was placed as a barrier between the water and the newly disturbed unprotected soils to exert the force necessary to keep the particles in place, to hold the foundation. There was something comforting about imagining millions of little downward forces, one for each grain of soil, keeping everything in place.

It was water that was the problem. Norman had come to see it as the enemy. No matter how well you designed something, water acted in adversarial ways. If you were trying to revegetate an area disturbed by construction, either there wasn't enough water so that the seed didn't germinate or there was too much of it and it washed away the seed and the soil you'd hoarded in long bench piles over the two-year project and then carefully spread back over the area. Water was crafty. It didn't behave and it even stole from the things around it. It leached minerals and drew off heat. It could even pilfer fundamentals, such as weight, as in Archimedes Principle, which stated that when a solid body is immersed in water, the loss in weight is equal to the weight of the displaced liquid. If you were trying to contain it, it always found a way through, or around, or under. As in the case of the bridge, the water was slowly, insidiously, cleverly eroding the structure's firm foundation.

That's why Norman was here now, standing under the green awning of Peccadillo's café—his wife's choice—waiting for her. He had sat in his ergonomic chair at the efficiently designed desk in his state-of-the-art cubicle for three hours trying to figure out the best solution to the bridge problem. There were just too many variables, too many things to consider. What design would be the most cost effective? The most reliable? The best compromise between the two? Norman's impulse was always to tear everything down and start from scratch, to do it right, but clients didn't want to hear that.

Norman checked his watch—12:12. Jasmine was late, as usual. Norman stepped out from under the awning to the curb and looked along the street, first to his left and then to his right. Cars came and went, people walked along the sidewalk, a bicyclist zipped across an intersection, but no Jasmine. Being late really bothered him. It was simply a failure of character. It showed a lack of control of one's life, one's time, as well as a complete disregard for another person's schedule. Norman put his hands in the pockets of his dress pants and jingled the keys, *kinkle-kinkle, kinkle-kinkle*. She should arrive soon. Once while waiting for her, Norman had calculated that she averaged approximately 17 minutes late.

Norman's marriage was a series of forces too, but these forces related to how strongly he or Jasmine wanted something or didn't want something, how hard they held their ground. J force—that's how he thought of the things Jasmine wanted— would sometimes directly counter his N force. Sometimes J force was stronger, especially when it came to their son Tom, and sometimes N force. Norman had to admit, though, by its very nature, N force tended to win out.

Ah, there she was, right on (late) time, her slender frame flowing smoothly through a group of college kids. Her movements were always loose-boned and languid, and her waist-length straight hair was so pale you could almost see through it. She was so beautiful. It always surprised him, how beautiful she was. Before Jasmine, he'd always been attracted to intense brown-haired women who ran marathons or their own businesses. These women always left him bewildered and slightly tired, as if he'd been asked to solve a Fourier transform without knowing what a Fourier transform was. But the first time Norman and Jasmine met, he'd felt washed clean, energized, buoyed aloft. She did that to him.

When he thought of his life before Jasmine, he thought of Galileo's Law of Inertia, which was also Newton's First Law of Motion—an object in motion tends to stay in motion unless acted upon by an outside force. Norman had been going through the motions, and then here came Jasmine, the outside force.

"Norman, I'm sorry," she said as she stood on her toes and kissed his cheek. "I had to drop Tom-Tom off at daycare, and then I got into my work and lost all track of time." She pulled her shoulders up to her ears and tilted her head sideways, a repentant little girl, and said, "You forgive me?"

Norman didn't answer. He noticed three pale strands of her hair hanging from the left sleeve of her black blazer—the one she always wore with jeans—so he reached out and plucked them off. This made her frown. She'd asked him not to do this in public, but he couldn't help himself. He frowned too. She looked away from him and down the street to where the light had just changed from green to red.

They both pulled back into formality. He held the door for Jasmine to walk through, and she said, "Thank you."

The hostess, a chaotic girl with dirty blonde dreadlocks springing like weeds from her head, hurried over and pulled two menus from the holder on the wall. "Just two today?"

"Three if you count the awkward silence," Jasmine said.

The waitress stopped and a blank look came across her face.

"No, just two," Norman said.

When they reached the table, he held the chair out for her. "I am but a sword in the hand of my empress," he said with a bow.

Jasmine's shoulders relaxed. "The perverse law of marital dynamics," she said and glanced back over her shoulder at him. He snorted.

The tension seeped from between them. Norman sat in his chair. He took a deep breath and let it out slowly.

They were seated near the kitchen, and to his left Norman could see through the doorway where the chefs like well-oiled machines were preparing food. Norman liked being able to see the kitchen. Everything was so clean and everybody so purposeful. He scanned right to the restaurant itself. It, however, was lunchtime chaos. Everyone talked loudly to be heard over the din, a woman in a business suit yelled into a cell phone, waiters and waitress rushed from one end of the restaurant to the other, people stopped and blocked the aisles. It all pressed in on him and made him feel as if he were in a whirlpool, so he focused back into the kitchen. That was better.

"So how is your day going?" Jasmine said as she glanced at the menu.

"Oh, you know."

"No. What?" Jasmine always asked, but she didn't really want to know. She wanted to hear that things were getting better, that things were fine. But sometimes Norman needed to talk about it.

"Well, the client on that project called this morning. Called me a shit engineer. He said, what kind of shit engineer designs an erosion control structure that fails within the first year?"

The guy was a real asshole. Norman tried to avoid his calls. He always started with, "You fucked up again" and then ranted for a half hour about how incompetent Norman was and how shoddy his work was, never mind that Norman only took over the project three months ago. Because this was a long-term client who gave Water Management LLC a lot of work, Norman had to grovel and say, "No, sir," and "Yes, sir," and "I'll do better next time." Hooke's Law of Elasticity—the amount something deformed under strain was directly, linearly related to the amount of stress. This client deformed Norman, all right. He always tried to steer the conversation to a solution, "Yes, sir, but we can fix this. It's do-able." But the man always cut him off in order to re-iterate how he'd already failed and why wasn't it done right in the first place.

Even though Jasmine nodded, she was only half listening. Norman could tell by the way her head bobbed just a little, like she was listening to music no one else could hear. She probably was. Jasmine was a trumpet player and composer, and she was always thinking about her music.

Norman admired her playing a lot. He didn't tell her—he wasn't sure why—but it was like she was the priestess of an ancient religion, and she worshipped daily. She was always mindful of it, and everyone always told Norman how well she played. She didn't play hard and staccato like those old jazz men. She could—but no, her compositions were fluid and soft and made up of repeating lapping refrains. It was as if the trumpet sound had turned into warm water.

Even though Jasmine was only half-listening, Norman kept talking. He needed to get it outside himself, like an impurity in the concrete that weakened its structure. "I didn't even do the design. It was Rosencrans, that guy they fired because he kept locking his keys in the car on the jobsite. That and other things."

"He said that? The client." Jasmine was watching him now, mildly interested. Her head was no longer bobbing.

"Yeah. This guy's a real piece of work. Steps on me whenever he can."

Jasmine glanced down at her hands and kept her eyes there. "I've been worried about you."

He knew she had been, the way she did everything before he even asked. The house was always clean when he got home from work. She got up with Tom when he cried at night, even when it was Norman's turn.

"What'll it matter in a hundred years?" Norman said.

Jasmine's jaw clenched. "I wish you wouldn't say that," she said. "It matters. It matters to you, to us." She gently slapped the table and bobbed her head. "It matters because it matters to you."

Norman flooded with gratitude. He knew she was going to say this because she always said it. And he needed her to say it because sometimes it didn't feel like it mattered at all, to anyone. His little life with his little job doing little designs that everybody took for granted. It didn't matter, in the larger scope of things. He didn't matter. But it meant a lot that he mattered to her.

"How was Tom when you dropped him off?" Norman said.

Jasmine smiled, and her eyes focused on a spot six inches above the middle of the table. "Do you know what he said? Every time we passed a house, he pointed and said, *buil-den, buil-den*. Did you teach him that?"

Norman shook his head and smiled. Just then, a harried waitress came and took their orders. Norman ordered a calzone. Jasmine ordered vegetarian spaghetti.

After she left, Jasmine said, "He's going to be a scientist, I just know it. He's always pointing out things and classifying them. He got your engineer gene." She hesitated and then said, "Let's hope it makes him happy."

Norman didn't respond and unrolled his silverware from his napkin.

She continued, "Not a musical bone in his body."

"I don't know," Norman said. "He seemed pretty musical this morning pounding on his tray."

She laughed, a genuine laugh, not an appeasement. Norman smiled. It made him feel good to make her laugh.

"Shows what you know about music," she said. "That wasn't music. That was pure curiosity to see if he could get that plastic bumble bee thing apart. Unsophisticated scientific method, but he was trying."

"He really does concentrate on things, figures them out."

"Yesterday he figured out how to get the top off his sippy cup."

Norman took a breath. He shouldn't say anything, but he did anyway. "This is going to make you mad, but I'm going to say it anyway. Please don't let Tom walk around with that sippy cup of water, please? He just drops it and dumps it on the floor and there's water everywhere."

"Norman, it doesn't hurt anything," she said. It was an argument they'd been having since Tom started walking. "He's thirsty. I give him a drink. If it gets spilled—"

"When it gets spilled."

"WHEN it gets spilled, we clean it up. No problem."

"YOU clean it up, because I won't let him have it."

"Did you ever consider that people are sometimes more important than messes? Why does it matter that a little water ends up on the floor?"

"It'll ruin the wood. Besides, he doesn't need to be walking around with water."

She was exasperated. "Let's not talk about this now. Did you come here just to pick a fight?"

He'd gone over the line. He shouldn't have said anything. "I'm sorry." He craned his neck forward and focused on Jasmine. "How did your work go this morning? Any further on that composition?"

She sat back in her seat and didn't say anything for a minute. She was considering whether she would forgive him. Then she shrugged a little and leaned forward. "You know how I was worried about my embouchure? Well, I think I've figured it out. I've developed a habit of tensing too much as I play. Trying to control it too much. Just plain trying too hard. Sometimes my shoulders ache by the end of a session. So this morning before I even picked up the trumpet, I stretched and did a few yoga poses to relax. Then, as I was playing, I made a concerted effort to relax, to keep my body and, most importantly, my lips loose."

"Uh-huh," Norman said. When Jasmine talked about her playing she sparkled like light reflecting off water. Her whole body leapt with joy, and her face animated.

"I could help you work that embouchure," he said and lifted an eyebrow. It was an old joke between them.

She smiled. "Wouldn't want to tire me out before the big game."

"That's right. Tomorrow's Saturday. The Jazzfest. I'm sorry. I completely forgot. I was going to work tomorrow. This project ..." Norman was so far behind he'd worked six weekends straight.

"What about Tom-Tom? You said ..."

"Well, maybe I could work just in the morning? Then you'll have the afternoon?"

"I've got to help with the arrangements—we'll call Patty. She'll babysit," Jasmine said, stone in her voice. Then, to soften things, she said, "There's something about being the only woman in the group. You end up doing the dishes, cleaning up the messes."

Not in our relationship, Norman thought but didn't say. It's me who keeps things clean, orderly. Sure, she cleans, but without me her life would be a mess. What he said was, "That's me at work. It seems like I'm always cleaning up someone else's mess."

The waitress brought their food. "Plates are hot," she said as she plopped them down on the table. "Get you anything else?"

Jasmine looked at Norman, and Norman shook his head. "No, thank you. I think we're good." Jasmine looked at the waitress and nodded her head.

After the waitress left, Jasmine leaned her head forward over her plate and narrowed her eyes, and some strands of her hair fell into her red sauce. Norman didn't say anything. "You know how long you been saying that?" Jasmine said in a low tone.

"What really gets me is I'm always two steps behind," Norman said. "I just can't wrap my head around this project. With other projects, I've been able to keep it all in my head. With this one, I can't." It was because they worked on a lot of sites for this client, and everything was an emergency. No sooner would he get one thing handled and the client would call about something else, something that should've been taken care of six months ago. The regulators were understanding for only so long.

"That's because you're always screwing with yourself," Jasmine said. "When a solution presents itself, you immediately think of something worse or bigger or some other problem. It's like you want to make sure you feel awful."

She really was just trying to help him, to fix things, to put things back in equilibrium. He knew that. Zeroth's Law—If two thermodynamic systems are each in thermal equilibrium with a third, then they are in thermal equilibrium with each other. That was the problem, his work was the third system, and it was not in equilibrium. It was pulling their systems out of whack.

"Mike and Billingsly don't help," Norman said. "Sure. Mike's a good engineer and he's supposed to be working for me on this project, but Billingsly's always pulling him to do other jobs. I'm supposed to be managing this, not doing the work, and I got nobody to do it."

"You have a hard time doing that anyway."

"Doing what?"

"Letting other people do the work. You'd rather do it yourself."

"It gets done right that way."

"Yeah, but you're a manager. You're supposed to be managing, not charging a hundred and twenty dollars an hour to plug in numbers."

"It's hardly just plugging in numbers."

She tilted her head. "You know what I mean." She was getting exasperated.

This made Norman feel better. He didn't know why he did this—drag her into his bad feeling—but it always made him feel better. "Let's change the subject," he said. "I think we should get Tom some trucks or tractors or something he can play outside with this summer. Some big ones."

Jasmine didn't say anything. She just looked at him and her jaw clenched.

"What?"

"Don't do that."

"What?"

"You ..." she hesitated and then because she hardly ever cussed she whispered, "*fucking* pull me into it, get me all riled up, and then you tra-la-la, let's talk about something else. No. Let's not."

"Jasmine. I'm sorry I brought it up. Let's just drop it."

"No. No. You brought it up. Let's talk about it." As she said this, her eyes intent on his, the left side of her face took on an orange glow. Norman glanced into the kitchen. A cook held a pan of flame in the air. Norman couldn't tell whether the cook had lit the dish on purpose or not, but he wasn't trying to put it out. He just stood there waving it in the air.

"Norman!" Jasmine hissed. "Are you listening?"

She was mad, really mad. He rarely saw her this mad. It was out of control. Newton's Third Law of Motion—for every action there is an equal and opposite reaction. He'd been thinking of his job being the action and her compensation as being the reaction, but now he saw that it was never just action-reaction. It was action-reaction-reaction-reaction, way on down the line. It eddied forever throughout their marriage.

"You've been bitching about your job and this project ever since you got it," she said. "You keep saying it's going to get better, but it's not. It hasn't gotten better."

"I ..."

"In fact, it's gotten worse. You work twelve-hour days and come home bitching and tired." Her eyes were shiny now. "I don't know what to do. When you talk about it, which is all the time, I try to offer suggestions, but they never help. I don't know what to say. How can I help? What am I supposed to say?" Her voice sounded like a trumpet solo, like one of those old jazz men, little punches of sound as they ran up and down the scales.

"Sometimes I just need to talk about it."

"So I'm just supposed to listen? How can I do that, just that?" She shook her head.

Norman didn't say anything. What could he say? That sometimes he needed to be rescued? Even if nothing came of it, it was enough that she tried. So he said, "Really, Jas, I really think it'll get better." It sounded lame, even to him.

"No, it won't. And I can't take it anymore. I might as well be a single parent. I give and give and still it's never enough. I keep the house clean because it usually helps you feel better— only it doesn't now. I short-change my music so I always take care of Tom-Tom and I try to have dinner on the table when you get home. It doesn't help though." She looked past him and out the plate glass windows. "What're we going to do?" She said it in a soft voice, not directed toward him. "Is it ever going to get better? No. I don't think so." When she said it, Norman's skin prickled. He extended his hands to bridge the distance between them, but Jasmine ignored them and continued looking out the window.

It was the law he hated, the Heisenberg Uncertainty Principle—the more precisely the position of a subatomic particle is determined, the less precisely the momentum at that instant can be determined. In other words, if you overdetermined—overcontrolled—the small things, you couldn't keep track of the whole or its future. There was just too much. What he hated about that law was that it wasn't a law at all. It simply said that there were no rules, everything was uncertain. Norman couldn't believe that. He just couldn't.

"Jasmine, please?" he said, his voice wavering. She looked from the window to him. Her eyes firm, she focused on his face for a long time. He kept his hands extended out to her, palms up, and unsupported they began to shake with the effort. Finally, she slowly extended her right hand. It was cool and dry in his hot moist palms. He closed over it. She gently placed her left hand on top of his and held, attenuating his uncontrolled trembling.

Snowshoeing

A SUNNY TWENTY-MINUTE DRIVE FROM LARAMIE to the Laramie Range on a winter's day to go snowshoeing. The roads are dry. No wind, for once. No ice on the interstate through Telephone Canyon, though there is on the two-track to the parking area. It isn't snowing now, but with puffy clouds like mounds of polyurethane foam it could go either way. The sun may stay out and it could get up to forty degrees, or it could start snowing in twenty minutes. The weatherman predicts partly cloudy with a thirty percent chance of snow showers, which is kind of a joke because thirty percent usually means there'll be snow.

Livie is glad she's wearing her driving gloves. A higher coefficient of friction provides a better grip on the steering wheel's leather cover. Her Subaru Forester's wheels are churning in the ruts of ice, even with all-wheel drive. Livie pushes in the clutch, grabs the stick, and downshifts. An automatic transmission is supposed to be better for continuous power and traction, but Livie likes the control of her manual.

"Just think about it," Mike, her husband, says from the passenger seat. He wants them to move south, California or Arizona maybe—if not for good, at least part time. They aren't at retirement age yet, but they've saved up enough to retire early. When they were first married, Livie made sure they invested the maximum in their 401ks, so that now, in their forties, they have a good nest egg. She's forty-five, and he's forty-four. Not enough, not enough, Livie thinks. What if they live past the 2011 National Center for Health-predicted standard life expectancy in the United States of seventy-eight point seven years? If they live into their late eighties or nineties, they won't have enough, and then they'll be too old to work.

He's forgotten to put on his safety belt again, but Livie doesn't bring it up because they're arguing. Not worth mentioning this time.

Dickens, their chocolate lab, lets out a low whimper from her crate in the back. She's nervous when they're arguing. If they were in their living room, Dickens would pace from Mike to Livie and then back to Mike, nosing their hands and whining.

Livie pulls into the Happy Jack parking area and maneuvers around the four-and-a-half-foot drifts of snow. She backs into a parking spot—she's read that you get into less accidents if you park with your tail end toward the curb, plus it's more practical to unload. She always gets irritated when she parks in this lot, though. Whoever designed the parking area didn't know what they were doing. It rests in a bowl below the surrounding terrain so that snow drifts across it, instead of being raised so that the wind blows it clear. The engineer also sloped the grade from south to north, even though drainage is designed to flow to the southern edge of the pavement, so that the northern half of the parking area is embedded in ice during the winter. The responsible party should have had to fix it, Livie thinks, even if it put them over bid.

Livie shuts off the engine and glances over at Mike. He's smiling as he says, "The fleecy clouds their chilly bosoms bare, and shed their substance on the floating air." He says it head held high, hand outstretched, emphasizing every word and rolling his *R*s dramatically. Livie can't help herself. She laughs. Dickens lets out a low woof from the back. The tension dissipates. Nothing is resolved, but everything is all right.

LIVIE AND MIKE MET AT THE UNIVERSITY OF WYOMING in Introductory Biology, a class of ninety-three students. Livie was fulfilling her life science requirement for her civil engineering degree, and Mike was in art at the time, although he was already taking a lot of English courses. He was interested in biological illustration, even though cameras made it obsolete. So like him, Livie always thought, to be interested in a technology that is one hundred and fifty years out of date.

Early in the semester, Livie sat in the front of the room— not the first row, which labeled you as the ultimate brown-noser, but in the second row where you caught enough attention to be thought of as a good student but not so much that you were eviscerated by the professor's stare. The second row was safe.

"Science is a process, not just a collection of facts," the professor said. "It's a series of techniques that, when used correctly, gives you a valid, scientifically sound, objective result. It removes the researcher's bias."

Livie wrote carefully in her notebook: "science = process ≠ facts only. series of techniques to get valid sci.-sound objective result. No bias." After class she would reread her notes and write in the margin, "Science is the same for everyone."

The professor glanced up the tiers of seats to the back of the room. Something caught his eye. "Yes?" he said. Livie twisted in her seat in time to see a tall skinny guy stand up. He was dressed all in black and his hair was dyed black and spiked in all directions. His hands were in his pockets and his shoulders slouched. He made Livie think of an awkward bird, a washed-out Audubon illustration with incorrect proportions that made you feel like your memories of birds weren't quite right.

"I get what you're saying," Guy in Black said. "But can you really say there's no bias in science?"

The professor snorted. Livie heard him because he was standing right in front of her. "We can talk about this after class, if you'd like," he said.

"No," Guy in Black said, "you're saying that science has no bias, but it has to. One person looks at a physical manifestation and gives his take"—at this point, the girl sitting next to him swatted his hip—"or her take," Guy in Black amended, "was what I was saying."

"An interesting philosophical discussion," the professor said. "Uh, what's your name?"

"Mike. Michael Wright." There was no shame, no hesitation in the guy's voice, no indication he felt he was disrupting.

"A discussion best saved for philosophy class, Mr. Wright. Now, as I was saying—"

"Don't you sometimes leave out results?" Mike said.

"No. Results are not intentionally omitted."

"Well, do experiments fail sometimes?"

"Yes, Mr. Wright. Experiments do fail. Now—"

Mike wouldn't let it go. "So that means you omit them. You don't mention them when you go on and do other experiments. Therefore, you leave things out, and that's bias."

"Mr. Wright, see me after class," the professor said and then continued his lecture.

How inconsiderate, Livie thought. Taking up the class's time for things that aren't important.

Everyone in the class was assigned a study group. Livie was in Mike's group, along with his girlfriend. The girlfriend was also an art student. She was a little heavy-set with big boobs. Mammary glands, Livie thought.

A couple of weeks later in study group they were talking about the cell. They sat in a circle. Livie sat two people away from Mike and opposite his girlfriend, whom Livie had begun to think of as Mammaries.

The grad student who led the discussion said, "A cell is the basic building block of living tissue."

Mike raised his hand. "Um, why is it called a cell?" he asked.

Him again, Livie thought.

He continued, "Why isn't it called, say, a ball, or a bubble? They all enclose and support." He turned his face away from Mammaries and smiled at everyone in the group. His teeth seemed whiter than they should be, and too big for his mouth. Something about his smile made Livie smile back.

"What?" the grad student said.

"I mean, a cell has negative connotations. Convicts live in a cell. Don't you think calling it, maybe, a womb would be more appropriate, more biological, more fair to the fairer sex?" He turned to Mammaries and tipped his chin down toward his chest, like an old-fashioned school marm looking over bifocals.

"Stop it," Mammaries said.

"See, Michelle and I have been having this discussion, and I thought you could resolve it for us." Mike smiled at the grad student, who looked nonplussed. "Michelle thinks that the metaphor doesn't matter, that the representation and the thing are the same. I was just pointing out that all representations have connotations." As he talked, he gestured with his hands. He had these long fingers, Livie noticed. To this day, all Livie has to do is think about those fingers and she'll have a sexual response. That's how she thought of it that day: How curious. I'm having a sexual response to this art geek.

Mike went on, "If you say in the newspaper that someone is a perpetrator, everybody'll think that they're guilty, whether they are or not."

"Mike, you're being an ass," Mammaries said.

Livie didn't like way she said it, like a scolding mother, so Livie said, "I think he has a point."

The grad student shook her head. "Labels are arbitrary, I'll grant you. But could you suspend disbelief just for this session?" She looked first at Mike and then at Livie.

"Do you concede that labels are arbitrary?" Mike said to Mammaries.

Mammaries raised her eyebrows.

"So it's agreed?" the grad student said. "It's a cell?"

Mike nodded. Livie nodded. Mammaries crossed her arms.

Livie understood why the girlfriend was exasperated, but for some reason she couldn't empathize with her. The next study session, Mammaries didn't show up, and by the end of the drop-add period, she wasn't coming to class. Livie and Mike started studying together. Soon they were a couple, and Mike switched to English as a major. They were married after they both graduated. Mike went on to get his master's in English and then hired on as a part-time and then a full-time Academic Professional Lecturer for the university. Livie got a job as a civil engineer and got her P.E., Professional Engineer's license.

MIKE OPENS THE HATCHBACK and lets Dickens out of her crate. She runs around the car sniffing here and there, her snout pulling her as if it were attached to a lead rope. She noses the snow and then drops her haunches and pees. She waddles forward as she finishes, butt to the ground, and then brushes her hind feet, first the left, then the right. The only other car in the lot sits in a two-foot drift. It's a copper-colored Camaro with one window taped over with silver duct tape and a garbage bag. There's a bright orange tag on the windshield wiper. How could you abandon your vehicle here? Livie thinks as she pulls on her coat and hat. It's been here long enough for the snow to bury it. What waste. What irresponsibility. Not to mention the taped-over window. A very poor solution to the problem.

"Wouldja look at that?" Mike says, pointing to the car with a ski pole.

"Umm-humm," Livie says and turns to retrieve her snowshoes from the hatchback.

113

"I used to want a Camaro so badly, in high school," Mike says. He puts down the pole and walks over to the car. He bends and scrapes the window with his glove and peers in. He turns to Livie. "What a cherry. It's got leather seats and everything."

"Were you going to carry the pack, and should I?" Livie says.

"Man, oh, man. There was this girl. Betsy Blondo. She drove a bright red Camaro. What I wouldn't've given to ride in that car." He sucks air in between his teeth.

"I'll carry it for a while," Livie says. She places her snowshoes on the packed snow and straps them on. Snowshoes are one of those inventions that never change. A marvel of early engineering. A long hoop with a system of mesh to distribute load across the snow so that the foot doesn't sink, and a pivot system so that the foot can rotate forward and backwards. They reached peak form in the 1800s. Does Livie know for a fact the 1800s? No. They could've been the same form in the 500s. The point is that materials are the only thing that's been improved. Aluminum has replaced the wood for the hoop and the leather for the pivots, and synthetics have replaced the leather of the mesh.

Mike returns to the Forester and straps on his snowshoes. "Let me get that," he says and takes the pack from Livie's hands. He swings it onto his back. They adjust their poles and pull on their gloves. Dickens runs up to them and bounces on her front paws. Then she turns and runs a ways away and then looks back. They walk through the opening in the pole fence and head off across the meadow. Its snow is packed hard, and the snowshoes slip like skis on its surface. Livie is careful where she places her feet. Half-way across the meadow, Dickens squats and poops. Livie pulls off her glove, pulls a plastic bag out of her coat pocket, and inverts it over her hand. She retrieves the poop, inverts the bag, twists it, pulls it over itself and ties it, so that it is double-bagged. She places it at the base of a bush. They'll pick it up on their way back and put it in the garbage can at the parking area. They enter the pine trees on the other side of the meadow. In front of them, a groomed ski trail climbs diagonally up along the ridge.

"Why don't we ever ski anymore?" Mike asks. Mike loves cross-country skiing, and he goes all the time with friends in the English department.

Livie doesn't hesitate: "Because you broke your leg, remember?" He had, trying to go off a jump. Or rather, landing afterwards. She nods her head for emphasis and smiles. Mike shakes his head back and forth. He sticks his left leg out straight and pretends to use his ski poles as crutches and pushes himself around in the snow. Livie laughs. Dickens hops up and down and then jumps up onto him, pushing him over into a snowdrift. Livie laughs harder. Mike pushes himself up and throws a stick for Dickens. She bonsais off into the snow to retrieve it. The real reason they don't ski, one that Livie'll never tell, is because Livie hates it. There isn't enough friction between the ski and the snow. Nothing to push against, no control. She tried it once. It was a disaster. It was ok when they were first out of the car on level ground. Shush-shush-shush as she put one ski in front of the other, sort of like slick snowshoeing. But her first out-of-control glide down a long slight slope was enough. Her whole body went rigid, which made her to go faster. Without making a sound, she screamed the whole way down. She tried to use her poles to stop and ended up punching herself in the gut. Then she curved off into the brush and smacked a tree. She was barely hurt, but it was enough for her to beg off.

Livie and Mike carefully cross the ski trail, trying not to leave deep imprints that would impede skiers, and climb the soft powder into the trees beyond. Dickens stops on the ski trail and looks up at them and barks once, short and sharp. She runs along the trail as they begin to ascend and then, resigned, she plunges into the powder and pushes her way through the snow to their trail and catches up with them. Mike is breaking trail. Each step he takes, his snowshoes are buried, and he sinks his poles deep in the snow for balance as he pulls first one snowshoe and then the other up from underneath its white weight. Livie's work is easier. She places her snowshoes in the holes Mike's have created, and she doesn't have to pull out of the deep powder. Still, they're going straight up the side of the ridge, and it's a lot of work. She starts to breath heavily. The cold air feels good in her lungs. She realizes she's been poling too much. Her deltoids start to tire. She consciously poles only every other step and her arms feel better.

Dickens plunges off into the deep powder, nosing at the base of trees and then returning to the trail. She bumps into Livie as she passes along the trail and moves to follow Mike up ahead. She looks back at Livie, her tongue lolling and her eyes smiling. The sun is out, and they move through patches of shadow and patches of sun. In a sunny patch, Livie stops to catch her breath. She looks up toward the top of the ridge, and the snow sparkles like an outfall of tiny diamonds.

She watches Mike as he moves. He looks the same as he did when he was twenty, Livie thinks. She knows that when he's naked his chest has a scooped out look, an old-man look, and he has high blood pressure, but here, today, it's a fine machine, all parts working smoothly and efficiently. He hasn't put on much weight. His shoulders are broad. Under his jeans, his thigh muscles round and then narrow near his knee. He's wearing gators over Sorels, the same gators he had when he was twenty. Livie likes the fact that they've lasted this long. It makes her feel like there's craftsmanship and continuity in the world. Livie thinks about that twenty-year-old boy. He was so earnest. He's gotten more cynical, more bitter with age. But today, she can see that boy he was, and it makes her ache for him. She wants to hold him close and protect him. Have I done all I can for him? she wonders. She's done her best to keep him safe, to make him comfortable, to ensure their future. Could she have done more?

Mike reaches the crest of the ridge and stops and turns. He cocks his elbows out behind and leans on his poles. "Come look at this," he says.

Livie digs in and climbs the hill. She stops next to him. On the other side, the ridge drops out from under them and they can see the vast valley beyond.

"Do you see that?" he asks.

She looks where he's pointing off down the valley. She squints against the sun. All she can see are the dark of the pines against the white of the snow and the blue of shadow on the opposite ridge.

"There. Can you see it?" he asks.

"No."

117

"An eagle. A golden. Right there." He shuffles over behind her and points over her shoulder past her ear. She thinks she can see something, a movement in the air of the valley below in front of the deep green of the trees, but it's not clear.

"It's gliding," Mike says. "The tips of its long brown wings are curling up in the wind as it banks and moves. She walks in beauty, like the night, of cloudless climes and starry skies." Livie hears him hold his breath and then let it out. "There, she put her head down. She's hunting for something."

There's the sound of the wind in the pines.

"I love you so much," Livie says. "Don't ever forget that."

Mike puts his arms around her and she leans back into him, feeling the warmth of his body. After a bit, they turn and climb along the ridge's spine toward a higher ridge, Livie breaking trail now. The slope gets steeper. The next time they stop, there's an empty bird's nest on an aspen branch at eye level. Livie marvels at how tightly it's constructed. The limber twigs are woven together like a thick small basket, and it appears to be caulked with mud. Think about how much work went into it. Livie wonders how it's connected to its supporting branch, what substance holds it so tightly. It must be mud, which is not known for its adhesive or elastic properties. The branch moves and sways but doesn't dislodge the nest. The nest must be balanced just so, and it must have been built over a period so that the mud had enough time to set like a natural cement. She's not at an angle to see.

Of good construction, Livie thinks, which makes her think of building their house.

IN THEIR EARLY THIRTIES, Livie and Mike decided to build a house. Nesting instinct, Mike joked, soon we'll have kids. Livie didn't see it that way. They'd lived in a series of run-down rentals, and it only made sense to stop throwing their money away. Not only that, but the layout of rentals never seemed logical, something she couldn't fix, and she was tired of fighting with landlords when things needed to be done. Building their own house meant they could get it right, have what they wanted.

They found some land up North Ninth out on Rogers Canyon, a beautiful grassy valley that opens up to the west with a view across the grassy high plains to the Snowy Range mountains beyond. They chose a spot sheltered from the bitter winds. This was before there were many houses in the area. They ran into trouble, however, when they applied for a bank loan. Mike wanted a grand house with a grate room and nothing but windows on the west so that they could watch the antelope and see the sunsets. He wanted five bedrooms for when they had kids and guests and a study for his writing. He wanted a deck around three-quarters of the house and landscaping of bushes and trees. He lit up when he talked about it. Livie didn't see the point of such extravagance, however. She wanted to make him happy, but they only needed three bedrooms, one for them, one for kids if they should have any, and one for guests. The guest room could double as a study, or he could use a corner of the living room. They could have a great room, but a full wall of windows wasn't energy efficient.

They fought bitterly about it. He argued that they were both professionals and they were making enough money to qualify for the loan. She argued that with the smaller loan they could pay extra and have it paid off in fifteen years. He countered by saying, what was the point. It might as well be a rental if that's all they were going to build. She didn't say anything to that, but with her stubbornness and her shear logic, she wore him down. They built the smaller house.

Livie was involved with every aspect of the building. It was something she excelled at, minding the details and managing construction. With the help of an architect friend, she designed the structure. She arranged for drilling the well and digging the septic system. She had electricity and gas run from the county road. She researched contractors and called references. Over the course of a summer, the stud walls went up and the roof beams were placed. When the dry wall contractor stopped showing up, she contacted a lawyer, and the dry wall was completed. It came together in the fall, their little house, within budget even. They moved in on September 1.

It wasn't Mike's dream home, but it was efficient and logically laid out. The kitchen, dining area, and living room were open to each other so that whoever cooked dinner could talk with whomever was in the living room. It had one and a half baths, water-saving toilets, and a high efficiency water heater. She put timers in the shower to help conserve water. There were windows on the southern exposure, but they shown in on a rock wall for passive solar heat. It was all on one floor, so when they were older and couldn't make it up the stairs it wouldn't be a problem. It did have Mike's porch to the west, though, and even on cold days, Mike would sit out and watch the sun go down, a wool blanket around his shoulders and a cup of tea in his hand. Now the area is a rich subdivision full of grand houses. Their little house looks like a garage next to these mansions. Livie can't say that she regrets it, especially now that the house is paid off, but sometimes she wonders if she did the right thing.

LIVIE AND MIKE COME TO THE EDGE OF THE PINES and into a shallow valley. Dickens runs on ahead. A frozen stream meanders down to a hollow. On the farther side of the hollow is a beaver dam and a beaver lodge. Beaver dams are a marvel of manual labor. A tree is felled and each branch gnawed through and dragged to the dam and carefully lodged where it will work the best, like a three-dimensional jigsaw puzzle. The lodge is like a little log cabin on the water. It provides enough insulation that two or three small closely packed bodies heat it comfortably. There's no water in the dam, though, no flat frozen pond, because the middle of the dam has been torn out, and the lodge is abandoned. Something about it makes Livie sad.

They move back into the trees. They come across another ski trail. They use its bridge to cross a frozen stream and then move back out into the trees and parallel the trail. Livie hears voices coming down the ski trail ahead of them. Dickens lets out a low woof. It's two women talking loudly.

"Do you know what he said to me?" one woman says. "He said you don't understand my needs. Can you believe it?"

"Really," the other woman says.

"Well, you can imagine what I said to him," the first woman says.

The women are close enough now that Livie can see their forms through the trees. Bounding ahead of them on the trail is a long-haired black dog.

Dickens takes a couple of steps toward the trail and lets out another low woof.

"Dickens, here!" Livie says. "Here!"

Dickens ignores her and starts moving toward the trail.

"Hey!" Mike says and stops Dickens in her tracks. She puts her head down and circles back behind Mike so she can see the trail and stands panting. Then she lets out a sharp bark. "Dickens!" Mike says. Dickens sits down on the back end of his snowshoes but keeps her eyes on the black dog as it runs past them down the trail.

Dickens always listens to Mike. She only listens to Livie if Livie gets mad.

The two women move off down the trail with smooth glides.

WHEN LIVIE WAS THIRTY-FOUR and Mike was thirty-three, Mike wanted to have kids.

They were lying in bed. "To use a cliché, your biological clock is ticking, my dear," Mike said. "I was reading that a woman's fertility starts declining when she's twenty-five, can you believe it?"

Livie pushed her butt into his crotch and wiggled it. She rolled over toward him and kissed his lips slowly and deeply.

He pulled his head back and said, "A man's fertility, though, it's going strong into his fifties." He has this little-boy I'm-so-proud-of-myself look on his face.

She reached down and pinched his nipple and tried to kiss him again. He took both of her hands in his and held them and kissed them.

"Don't you want to have kids?" he asked.

"It only stands to reason that a delicate system such as reproduction would decline. Not to mention evolutionarily humans are best able to take care of young when they're in their teens," she said and pushed her breasts into his face. He let the matter drop.

The next time he brought it up, Livie said she'd think about it. The third time she went to her gynecologist. Secretly, she hoped he would tell her that she was too old to have children. The gynecologist gave her a full exam and told her that, as far as medical science was concerned, she could have twenty babies. She didn't tell Mike though. She weighed her options. It didn't make sense to have a baby. They were well on their way to financial security. Their life was good. Why change it? They were happy. They could take care of themselves in their retirement. Plus, it was selfish to bring a child into this already-overpopulated planet.

But she didn't tell Mike any of this. She kept putting him off. He insisted they talk about it. Finally, she did something that to this day made her insides curl like burned paper every time she thought about it. She told Mike she had fieldwork to do and would be gone for a week. She went to a doctor in Denver and had her tubes tied. Then she told Mike that her gynecologist said she wouldn't be able to have kids because she was in premature menopause. Mike was shocked at first and then was very supportive.

"Don't beat yourself up about it," he said.

The clouds are piling up over the Laramie Range as they climb the steep slope. Dickens is tired now and follows Mike closely in his tracks. She doesn't venture off into the powder. Once, Livie has to hold onto a slim tree to keep from slipping.

123

They push to the top of the ridge and come out onto the peak. In one direction they can see all the way to Laramie, and in the other they can see Vedauwoo, huge granite rock formations that thrust from the ground like an alien city. Dickens lays down between them and gnaws at the snow stuck to her front paws.

Mike looks off toward Vedauwoo. "Are you sure you won't think about moving, Livie?" Mike says.

Livie glances toward Laramie. It doesn't look like much from here, houses spread out across a broad grassy plain between two mountain ranges. She can see the dome of the Arena-Auditorium and the teepee of the American Heritage Center. "But we live in Laramie," she says. "Everything we know is here."

"Yes, precisely." Mike gently pokes her with his ski pole. "Everything we've known for twenty-five years."

"Twenty-seven years," Livie says automatically.

Mike shakes his head. "Yeah, twenty-seven years."

"If we move, we'll have to start over."

"Not start over. Just change. Adapt. Think of it as an evolutionary imperative."

Livie doesn't say anything. She feels paralyzed.

"Live a little, Livie," Mike says.

Dickens's whine starts low and gets louder, more insistent. Then it's loud and punctuated and short: uuuh, uuhh, uuhh. She gets up and moves first toward Mike and then toward Livie.

"Mike—" Livie says

But before Livie can say anything, he blurts, "I set up a post office box. I meant to tell you. So I'll have a permanent address for submissions. If we move, I mean." He keeps his eyes turned toward Vedauwoo.

A single snowflake like a cinder falls between them.

There it is, that thing that always stalks her on huge soft paws, that unnamable monster. When she buys groceries, it's there. Is their diet balanced enough? Do these vegetables have pesticides? When they drive in the car, it's there. Is that other driver drinking? Is that trucker running on No-doz and lack of sleep? Is he drifting into her lane? When she pays the bills, it's there. Will they have enough money? Has she budgeted well enough? When Mike develops a cough, it's there. Is he getting sick? How's his blood pressure? Always, it's there. What is she forgetting? What hasn't she planned for? Circling, circling, eyeing her, crouching and panting, it is there, always there. Panic grips Livie's throat and almost shakes her from her feet. She pushes on her poles to steady herself.

He has a secret. It's not just a post office box. It's his post office box, his alone. She would not receive her mail there, and she has no control over the mail he receives. It is the first step in creating a new life, one that may or may not contain Livie. Livie feels Mike's identity split off from hers like a piece of kindling under the woodchopper's axe. They are not a *they*. She is Livie and he is Mike. She looks back at Laramie and then toward Vedauwoo. She looks at Mike. She sees the young man he was and then his age draped over him like a pall. There is a distance between them she's never felt before. She sees the set of his shoulders and wonders, will this be it?

Snow starts to fall, big fluffy flakes that catch on eyelids and melt into the hair and threaten to cover you with its soft insistence. "Where was it you'd like to move?" she asks, closing the distance between them and grasping at his sleeve, as the snowfall erases the tracks behind them.

In the Headlights

THE SUN WAS WELL BELOW THE HORIZON, and the hills like herds of nibbling rabbits were silhouetted in blue-white relief. Packets of heat rose from the red dirt hardpan near the road, and it was like moving through clothes hung from a summer clothesline—cool, warm, cool, warm. There, a breeze on my skin, brushing the hairs on my arms, fanning the back of my neck, which was sticky with sweat. Now and then, the breeze played with the power line on the ridge, an eerie buzzing, twanging sound like my every last nerve at its breaking point. One lone cricket went *chirrup, chirrup, chirrup* and then went silent. I could smell the heat, the dry baking of clay, the pungence of juniper, and, every once in a while, just a whiff of the green lushness of the creek bottom—cottonwood and cattail and succulents—a mile away. When I smelled that, I wanted to be there in its solid coolness, cupped and protected from the scorching dry heat. I wanted to give up and go home.

Was that headlights?

No.

I walked, feeling my way. In the dark, I had no perspective—I couldn't see the ground, I couldn't distance things.

Through the thin soles of my tennis shoes, I felt small rocks, some smooth and round, some sharp and jagged, poking the bottoms of my feet. I put my foot forward again and right there was a big lump, round and hard. My right foot rolled sideways off its back. The bones on the outside of my ankle pushed together hard and the tendons on the inside of my ankle pulled and gave just a little. My leg was forced straight and the stretch extended through my achilles and up my leg. I pitched forward and dragged my left foot through the gravel to catch myself, making a low rasping noise with my foot. Then I fell forward onto my left foot, my weight dropping and my knee punching my chest. I froze, my right foot drawn up from the ground. I thought, Damn, that's going to hurt, and sure enough, with a second's delay, there it was, a sharp stab and then a throbbing.

What was I doing out here in the dark? Why had I set this up?

Because I was fifteen and he was nineteen. Because he said once, "I thought of you the other day," and because he was the only one I knew who repeated things I said after I said them, as if he actually heard what I said and valued it.

Before I left the house, I had washed my face with a washcloth that smelled like a field of wheat. At first it was all rough stiffness from being dried on the line, and then I wet it under the faucet and it melted, its fibers softened by the water. I rubbed it hard against my cheeks and my eyes, and I washed my neck and behind my ears. I rewet it and wiped inside my ears with the motion of a question mark. Leaning forward with my hip bones pressed hard against the bathroom counter, I dusted my cheeks with blush, a shade closer to fish meat than peach flesh, and I applied mascara, feeling the brush scratch against the edges of my eyelids. I combed my rodent-brown hair and shook it. I'm not much, I thought—nose like the sinking Titanic jutting from the middle of my flat wide face, eyebrows patchy arches, mouth a wide thin arc. My face was inches away from that other face, the one that stared back at me unflinchingly, the ugly one. I tried to pull back and see that face like I imagined other people saw it—innocently, without the knowledge of ugliness, but I couldn't, so I turned away.

But in the dark, it doesn't matter if you have on mascara and blush. You can't see yourself in a mirror, and other people can't see you either. You are you in your essence. People can't judge you. They can only hear you or, if they're close enough, feel you.

Was that headlights?

It was. I could see the reflection of lights on a red hillside a mile away as a car turned the corner. The narrow shadows of bushes slid across the cupped red surface like the pointer of a sundial, starting at the left and lengthening, lengthening, pulling right and right and lengthening until they peaked, long and slender and straight, and then shrinking, pulling to the right and widening.

Something bubbled in my chest and pushed hard up against my breastbone and then punched up through my throat and into my mouth. It tasted bitter and salty and metallic. I tried to swallow, but the bubble blocked my throat so I forced it down. I swallowed hard and it hurt.

The car came around and then there were the lights, first one then the other, cutting through the darkness like a fish knife. They shone in my eyes—from the top of the hill up there

129

across the valley to here where I was silhouetted on top the next hill. I was in the headlights. I wondered if he could see me standing there in the middle of the road waiting for him. I lifted my hand to wave but then the light fell away as the car's front end dipped down and it began its descent into the valley. For a moment, I stood there in the pitch black in the middle of the road with my hand raised.

The car began to descend the hill, its lights' long trace illuminating the paleness of the road. The brakes squeaked, first a couple short squeals and then a long low whine. The car eased down the hill, the engine moaning low as it surged a little at the restraint of the brakes.

The lights showed a long flat paleness but then there was movement at the edge. If I'd been in the car I knew what I would've seen: two pale green lights like tiny flashlights right there at the edge of the road. Something was there, something small and furry with its little heart beating fast in its chest, *thumpa-thumpa-thumpa-thumpa*, and its tiny chest pushing out and pushing in and its breath coming fast in its lungs. It was there at the edge of the road like a rock in a slingshot pulled back as far as quivering little arms could do. It sat stock still but with all the potential in the world.

I wanted to yell out now, No! Don't do it, even though I knew they always did. They always let the fear and the confusion of the huge roaring lights get to them and make them run. They never ran away though. Why did they always run toward the lights? Why were they drawn to the roaring horror?

My body tensed and my stomach balled into a fist as I pushed out into the darkness toward the animal. Don't do it, don't do it, don't do it—I tried to push the words out there through all that space and resistant darkness. Then I heard someone talking, whispering low and quick, "Don't do it, don't do it," and I knew it was me.

There was a moment right before you shot a rabbit when you saw it down the long black length of the twenty-two—the animal's head like a dandelion puff, its ears up and then one flipping back and forth like it was trying to shake off a fly and then the little eye so introspective like it was thinking about what it was going to have for dinner and its jaws back and forth working on a grass stem. You saw this framed by the dark square of the gun sight and for a minute you thought, this is an animal and I'm an animal and we're both thinking about what we want for dinner and in another world we'd sit together side by side and eat grass and flip our ears at the flies. But it wasn't that world—it was this world. That wasn't another animal like me. That was food and nothing more than a bale of hay with a sheet of typing paper pinned to it with a big circle drawn on it and then a little circle, all in black felt-tipped pen.

Then I saw the quick movement as the animal pushed off from the edge of the road. I imagined the strong back legs pressing against the ground and pushing the dust back in a little puff like the Road Runner, a cartoon cloud for such an innocent move. All the animal had to do was sit there, though, sit still, push the fear down deep inside it and wait, not move, not act, just stay, and the roaring horror would pass it by. But no—it kicked hard against the ground and pushed itself forward to get away from the *thumpa-thumpa-thumpa-thumpa* and the terrible air ballooning in its chest.

It jumped two quick jumps forward and then it dodged away from the car and ran down the middle of the road. The little form jerked forward as if attached to a string some kid yanked as he ran. Forward, forward, forward, the little animal raced and pushed ahead of the lights and toward the cool dark. The distance between the lights and the animal lengthened, its jerky movements and its fear propelling it faster.

But the car was on an incline and it coasted forward, first slowly but then more quickly as gravity took ahold and pulled it down. The brakes didn't squeak but the engine didn't rev either, no pushing of the car to catch the little bounding shadow.

That made me feel soft inside. The boy in the car wasn't stomping his foot on the gas trying to run the animal down. Some boys would do that. They'd stomp down on the pedal and aim the car like it was a gun. Not because they were hungry. Not because they were defending themselves. No. Because they could. Because it was the power over another living creature and they couldn't help themselves. They couldn't let power just be. They had to use it.

No. This boy just eased down the hill and the little animal ran out ahead of him, like they were playing tag. You can't catch me, you can't catch me. I wanted to be sitting next to the boy then. I wanted to feel the muscles of his thighs under my hand as they tensed to move from the gas to the brake. I wanted to play with the inseam of his jeans and flick it with my fingernails. In the darkness of the cab, I wanted hear his voice come to me in its low raspiness.

That was why I was standing in the dark—to feel the heat of his body against my arm and know that he could feel the heat of mine and the heat would come together between us and become one temperature, one heat.

The little animal's path took it back toward the side of the road. It's going to make it, I thought. It's going to angle off the road and with one long bound it'll jump into the borrow ditch and be gone, off into the enfolding safety of darkness. My breath came out in a whoosh of air and then I realized that I'd been holding it in, gripping it with the velvety hooks of my lungs and squeezing it tight. I took a long breathe to replace the sagging emptiness and then another and felt the buoyancy of oxygen as it entered my blood. It was going to be all right.

But the little animal couldn't let it go. It couldn't let itself be drawn away from that horrible roaring light. In an instant, it dodged toward the center of the road. Now it ran parallel, sideways to the lights, and for an instant I could see its sleek silhouette, ears tucked tight like an aviator cap against its neck and front legs tucked up against its belly as it leapt, its hind legs trailing long and loose as it arced through the light.

It can still make it, I thought. One more clean jump and it'll clear the edge of the road and be gone. My fists clenched against my thighs and I tapped my leg, tap-tap-tap-tap. My jaw clenched too, so I opened it wide and sucked in the black air and felt it cool on my tongue and then the inside of my throat. You can do it, I thought.

But the little animal couldn't let it go. What must it feel? On three sides, the cool inviting blackness, safety quietly beckoning, but on the other side roaring evil light bearing down on you. Why can't you let the darkness enfold you, gently pull you away? Why can't you look away from that horrible light and see the darkness and let it draw you? But you can't. The horrible roaring light has your eyes, your ears, your legs, your heart. You can't let it go.

The little animal took one last jag directly toward the car. I saw it, a little black dot, one more time before it disappeared between the headlights. Under the soft purr of the engine, did I hear a small thump? Or was it only anticipatory imagination, a phantom sound I sensed psychically more than anything? But the rabbit was gone into the blackness behind the light.

All of a sudden I was afraid. The car reached the bottom of the valley and the lights swept up the road like the searchlights of Alcatraz. I heard the roar of the engine as the boy pressed on the accelerator to force the car up the hill. The lights swept toward me and soon I'd be enveloped and pinned. Soon he'd be able to see me in those horrible lights.

I stiffened. With my torso, I could almost feel the warmth of the boy's body and of his voice. I imagined the soft interior of the car and the seat's pressure against my thighs and my butt and my back and the way the light from the dashboard and the headlights glowed on the contours of his face. But my legs could feel the cold reach of those lights like a million horrible hands grasping for me to hold me and pull me down into that unknown behind the lights, that horrible painful pressure squeezing the life out of me.

The roar got louder and louder. The lights crept up the hill. They were almost on me.

My legs took over and I bolted. I felt the bumps of rocks through the soles of my shoes as I turned and pushed off and tried to escape those lights. They touched my feet as adrenaline shot through me and I jumped high and wide, a standing long-jump, away, away toward the darkness of the borrow ditch. I came down and pushed off again against the hardness of the road and then I felt the ground buckle and give way as I landed in the soft enfolding dirt of the shoulder. My feet sank and dirt mounded up over my shoes and onto my ankles and sifted around my feet, dragging me down. I pushed off one last time and leapt, both feet in the air and pulled up and then extending down. I landed, my knees bent to scoop up my weight, and once I'd gathered myself, I twisted my body around to see the car.

It didn't slow. It didn't stop. The roaring blasted around me and through me and terror held me twisted and stiff as the lights swept behind me and collapsed into the darkness and the roaring of the car. Then the roaring was gone and the car was surrounded by a halo of reflected light. I could see the hard dark outline of the hood and the sides and I could see the light reflected through the windshield and the inside of the car and through the back window to me.

I saw his head, a little oval of blackness against the harsh square of light. Just his head. It was framed by the dark square of the seat back. His eyes were focused forward into the light, he was blinded, and I was back here in the safe enfolding darkness, the darkness behind the light. He was gone, and I couldn't catch him.

The Body Animal

THE FIRST TIME SYLVIA NOTICED SOMETHING WAS WRONG, she lay in her small bed off her parents' room. She was nine years old. As she lay there alone in the dark, she could hear the crickets chirping out her window, and she could feel the breeze from the window ruffling the hairs on her arms.

Even though she couldn't put words to it at the time, she was aware of her thoughts drifting from one thing to the next. She felt her thoughts skate over the sensations in her body: "This is a cool breeze, the sound of crickets, the refrigerator kicking on and humming, the dog's nails clicking on the wood floor." She was relaxed and did not move, and she felt her body.

All at once, her flesh seemed to fall away, not to exist, and she was nothing more than a network of nerve fibers extending into space like tree branches. She followed her left leg's nerves down to her toes. She could feel the pressure of the bed against the back of her leg, but she couldn't feel her toes. She knew that if she moved them she could, but she didn't want break this spell. Her nerves felt gossamer, a spider's web but sturdy and supple like wire. Then she was aware of how separate her thoughts were from her body. The thoughts didn't seem to originate in her head. Instead, they seemed to buzz around her eyes and ears in a separate dimension from her body—not totally apart but somehow disconnected, somehow ancillary and derivative of sensations from the physical, like shadow or coolness, part of her body but their own world as well. Her thoughts could be within her body and about her body but then they could ignore her body and go completely to that other dimension of her mind.

She thought of the dog—Collette, the golden retriever. She thought about how the dog was so physical, smiling with its whole shivering body, fetching sticks, focusing just on her, her little sister Daphne, her mother, or her father. The dog didn't pretend to know things on her own—she always looked to them. Collette was careless about Sylvia's commands, but she always listened to Daddy's. When Daddy and Sylvia went for walks with Collette, the dog was like an extension of Daddy. He asked her to go forward, to stop, to sit, and to roll over, all without a leash. Collette lived for it.

Collette was just like Sylvia's body. Sylvia's body always listened to her commands. It came when she called and obeyed her even more than Collette did. It obeyed her like Collette obeyed Daddy. So Sylvia began to think of her body as her pet, with her thoughts as master. She really resided in her thoughts, and her body was the faithful beast of burden.

Thus, she named her body "my body animal."

Another night, lying in the dark, Sylvia wondered whether her mind could affect her body—her mind feeding her body impulses like her body fed her mind. She tried an experiment. She imagined that there was someone standing next to her, her sister perhaps, who stroked the skin on her right arm. She imagined every detail—how the touch was light and soft, the heat from the person, how the person had a hangnail that scratched against her skin. The hairs on her right arm prickled, and the place where she had imagined the strokes felt warm. Her body animal appreciated being petted.

Sylvia tried another experiment. She had seen Daddy throw the ball for Collette for hours, till Collette's tongue wagged like her tail, yet she still wanted to retrieve the ball. Was Sylvia's body as compliant as Collette? Was her mind really the master? She decided to test it. She chose a cool day with low gray clouds that promised rain—but not too much rain. She ran around their small block. Her stiff limbs became supple and joyous in their movements. They loosened as if lubricated. She felt like a well-tuned engine, levers and cogs shifting and circling in predictable patterns—*ka-sshhh, ka-sshhh, ka-sshhh*. The second lap, Sylvia felt the motion of her legs and arms, and then her pounding feet seemed to lift from the uncompromising gray surface. Her body animal was a bird, and her pistoning legs became wing beats, each push feathers against the hard air. She was elated. The third lap, her legs and arms began to tingle. She liked this feeling. The hair on her body stood on end, and the air around her vibrated and pulsed. The fourth lap, she began to tire. Her body and her lungs felt strained, like wet sails. The air offered more resistance. "No," she told herself, "no, I won't be tired," and she urged her animal on. The fifth lap, she wanted to quit. Her body animal whined in agony. Her running muscles like taunt rubber bands felt hot in the thighs and cold in the calves. Her elbows dripped sweat from their creases.

Her body animal whispered and whined to her mind: "Why are we doing this? Why are you punishing us? We didn't do anything wrong." Her mind answered, "Well, that's true. My body animal didn't do anything wrong. We could stop now," and she began to slow. "No!" She caught herself. "My mind is master. We'll keep running." After a bit, her body asked, "But why? What's the point? You know, you could just walk for a little bit, just a little, just to the post up there. Then we could run again." It was seductive and wheedling, this voice. Sylvia found her mind saying "Yes, that's true. Why not? Just to that post." Then she caught herself again. "No!" She kept running.

Soon the burning stopped. Pain and exhaustion waned in the sixth lap. Her body animal quit whispering to her and bent to its task. Then it felt like a tool again, a well-oiled machine, but this time without either the joy or the pain. Her body animal was performing its function and performing it well. Her movement was fluid, as if her joints could bend in all directions and the repetitive motion could go on forever. When she came around the corner on her seventh lap, Momma stood in the driveway. "Sylvia," she said, "quit fooling around and get dressed. We have to go." Sylvia wanted to run past her mom, to keep going, to run on and on. But no, she wouldn't. Now she knew: her mind was the master of her body animal.

This realization made Sylvia feel invincible. Now she climbed trees and played soccer with the boys in the park. She helped Daddy change the oil and spark plugs. She took ballet lessons. Her body was her own. It was her animal, her playground, her kingdom, and she ruled that kingdom with a fair but firm hand. When her body animal was tired, she let it sleep; when it was hungry, she fed it; when it was restless, she ran.

Slowly, gradually, though, things changed. In high school, the girls told her she looked fat. "You're as big as a horse," they said as they whinnied and laughed. "Heee-eee-eee!" Sylvia looked at TV and in magazines and discovered, yes, her body was big. It had hard muscles that bulged in her butt and arms. Her thighs curved like smooth stones. Now, though it was the same, her body animal seemed altered. It had betrayed her. She had thought it subdued and obedient, but it was not. It undermined her authority and made her ugly.

"But, even though it's been disloyal, I will forgive it," she told herself. With faith in her mind's mastery, she began to deny her body animal. When she was hungry, she did not eat. Instead, she filled her body with motion. She joined the track team, and the 10K was her distance. She ran and ran. She stayed after practice, pounding down the darkening track. In the evenings, she fell into bed exhausted. In the mornings, she woke and her body animal groaned and growled, but she ignored it. She started drinking coffee to satisfy it, or she went for a morning run. She lost weight rapidly and was pleased with her success. Yes, she thought. It fortified her belief that her mind was master of her body animal. She became popular at school with her physical metamorphosis and her success in track.

But her body animal undermined her efforts. Its voice niggled and nagged. It would try reason: "You must eat to live, to fuel your motion, if you want to continue and be successful at track." When that didn't work, it became more devious: "Just one bite. Just one more. That's all we need. What can one little bite hurt?" Or it would say: "See that skinny girl over there? She's eating a candy bar. If she can do it, why can't we?" The voice became more persistent. It muttered around her ears, and she wanted to bat it away like a horsefly.

One day during a race, it felt as if jagged teeth ripped her right calf. She collapsed into a pile on the asphalt, the other runners tripping over her. Her leg throbbed, and it felt numb and burned. She writhed, and her body animal screeched its agony so that Sylvia couldn't think. She sat on the asphalt and her senses seemed to pull up like a party favor and roll into her body. Zooooouuuuuup! She fainted. Later she found out that her heel had suffered a stress fracture from the continual pounding and her achilles tendon was slightly torn. "You're also dehydrated and anemic, and you seem to be vitamin-deficient," the doctor said. "You need to take better care of your body."

"Body animal," she silently corrected.

The doctor said "your body" as if she were this one thing, this unity, this self that inhabited one space. As if the self and the body were the same thing.

She began to doubt her body animal. Before it was the faithful packhorse of her mind—now it failed to carry the burden and would not obey her rein. She tried not to think about it, even though it was always there. Because she couldn't run and because the doctor and her mother put her on a strict diet, Sylvia began to gain weight, just a little at first but then more. She developed curves where there had been bone, she felt her flesh get in the way as she bent and moved, her belly felt like an inner tube when she sat, and her thighs rubbed as she walked on her crutches. The flesh on her arms swung wide and loose like Jell-O on her bones. She was clumsy, too, where once she had moved like liquid.

She felt way too big. "This isn't my body animal," she told herself. "This is an alien that hangs on my bones."

But as she developed these curves and sat in the front porch swing sipping sour lemonade, the boy who lived across the street came over to talk to her. At first, he always had an excuse. "Umm. My mom was wondering if your mom was playing Bunko tonight?" "Umm. Did you see our cat?" "Umm. Do you have a cup of sugar?" Soon, though, he didn't make excuses and climbed right up on the porch and sat on the railing.

Sylvia resented these intrusions at first, but then she got these strange feelings. He turned up her walk, and her body animal took an involuntary breath and her nipples and groin tingled. Her face flushed. That little voice took over her mouth and said inane things and giggled. Soon it felt like she was all flesh and body—her body animal had taken over, and her mind went on holiday. Her body animal invited the boy to sit on the swing next to her because it wanted to be next to his body animal. Her body animal felt overwhelming, and even when the boy wasn't around, it would go sinuous at the thought of him.

The first time he kissed her, her mind went away completely. That ethereal plane that she inhabited most of the time extinguished with a *pop!* like a computer monitor. Suddenly she was totally body, with hormones surging like tides through her veins and brains. At once, her body animal didn't feel huge and clumsy—it felt like it inhabited the space that it was supposed to. Then she wanted her body to get bigger and bigger, to be big enough to take in the whole world and this guy, whose lips felt like velvet. She wanted time to stop. The next morning, though, she felt like she had gone insane. She was back on that cozy plane of the mind. She couldn't remember what had made her feel and act so inanely—like an animal, like a dog bitch in heat, like a cat that paced the house and yowled at night.

"No," she told herself, "I'm not going to be that."

She told the boy to go away and graduated from high school shortly after. She began to attend a nearby liberal arts college and declared her major as philosophy. She found college to be heaven on earth. She continuously lived on that plane of her mind, and she found other people who lived there too. She read books and fell in love with authors. Her health returned and she started running again, but this time she took it easy. She didn't worry about what she ate. She didn't have to—life and ideas were her food. She forgot her body animal.

Right before graduation, she was forced to think about the future. She met a guy in one of her philosophy classes whose thoughts were akin to her authors, so they decided to get married. They were a committed couple, but their sex life was almost nonexistent. That was the reason Sylvia had married him—because he didn't make her feel like that boy across the street. He didn't threaten her mind's superiority over her body.

Sylvia rarely let her body animal out of its cage. But things happen, as they do, and soon she was pregnant. She hadn't planned it, and she was surprised when the doctor told her. How could this be? So she tried to be conscientious in taking care of her body animal. She told herself that nothing would change after the baby was born. She and her husband would still go to book discussions and sleep in on Saturday morning and eat toast and tea while reading the paper. But her body animal reasserted itself. It began in small ways: her joints became so loose that she clicked as she walked. She became exhausted. Then her stomach grew thorns and scraped her insides continuously. Once again, her body animal got larger and larger, and there was nothing she could do about it.

Sylvia resented it all and wished it would all go away. The life growing inside her didn't seem real. Instead, it felt like once again her body animal had revolted, and this time it enlisted everyone around her. Her husband was oversolicitous, neighbors talked about the glory of motherhood, and complete strangers walked up to her on the street and put their hands on her belly. Her body animal had become community property. People discussed her organs and her sex life as if she weren't in the room. Doctors looked at parts of her body animal that she had no notion of. The only private place she had was the plane of her mind, that place she had always believed would come first. That place where she could go away and somehow be clearer, purer, more real than the world itself. So she withdrew and went there as much as possible. She began keeping a journal and writing long incoherent poems. But the body animal part of her world pressed her mind plane so much that she couldn't even breathe.

Then one day something inside her rolled over like a fat poodle and she began to bleed. She miscarried in the sixth month. That body animal of hers that was so bent on expanding, putting forth, reproducing, and inhabiting the world, gave up. Pain wracked her body and reduced the world to its locus in her abdomen. She cried and curled in a ball on the carpeted floor, heat pad to her belly, TV droning in the background. Then she slept.

Her body animal was a paradox, she thought afterwards. It wanted to take over her world, to take it all in, to devour it, and to populate it. To take in or take over. Yet it rejected her—her mind plane—in the process. It tried to punish her with pain and hunger, and when it got its way it balked. It was perverse. It was a sullen ungovernable creature.

Soon as she had recovered, she left her bewildered husband and moved to another state. She got a job as a waitress in a breakfast place and tried to sort things out. Soon, though, she quit going to her job altogether and never left her apartment. She spent weeks at a time in the same blue velour sweat pants and Mickey Mouse T-shirt. She only went out to get food, which wasn't often because she didn't eat much. At first her boss called once a week, then every day, then not at all.

To pass the time, she surfed the net on an ancient laptop. She followed meandering paths through intellectual thickets. She reread the Wikipedia entries of eighteenth century philosophers. She researched the history of coffee houses. She became fascinated with the social rituals of African tribespeople. She read that a tribe was introduced to Shakespeare's *Hamlet*. Rather than being overwhelmed with its universality, the tribespeople didn't understand it. "Of course, the man should marry his brother's widow," they said. This led her to reread the play, and the "To Be or Not to Be" speech rung her like a bell.

Then she went back on the internet to do research on the best way to die. Definitely not hanging or drowning—she imagined it would be like dying of claustrophobia. Statistics said that a gun was a good way to go, but she wasn't sure how to get one, and besides, what happened if she weren't killed? Trapped in a body animal in hell and unable to complete the job. Besides, it would be painful. Some said freezing to death was a good alternative—they said it felt like going to sleep— only it was summer and she couldn't wait. The ideal thing would be lethal injection. Doctors argued that it was a humane alternative to the electric chair. It would be like going under anesthesia. But she knew no doctors nor much about lethal injection. If not this, then another drug? The thought figuring dosages overwhelmed her—too little and nothing happens, too much and the body throws up and nothing happens. She finally settled on slitting her wrists. It was really the only option. She had a bathtub, she had a reasonably sharp paring knife, she had water, and who cared who found her? She wouldn't know whoever it was, and to them she'd be just another empty shell. A little pain, she'd felt worse.

First she burned her journals and threw almost everything she owned into the garbage. It wasn't much, a few books, some clothes, some toiletries, the laptop. She threw it out on Thursday morning so that it would be picked up that day. Jane Doe was as good a name as any.

She went to the kitchen and got the knife. She went to the bathroom, laid the knife on the stool lid, and turned on the faucets. She loved warm baths. This would be good. She poured in gardenia bubble bath, a throwaway packet from a hotel. She thought it might hide the color of the water, at least until she didn't care. She got into the bath with her clothes on and let the water run and the bubbles mound over her. She lay back and closed her eyes.

When the tub was full, she turned off the faucets and moved the knife to the side of the tub. She lay back again and closed her eyes. It felt good. Her body animal relaxed. She cleared the bubbles a little and slid down so only her nose was above the water. She imagined the color red behind her closed lids. The red turned to orange. She lay for a long time. Like when she was a child, her flesh seemed to fall away from her body. Even her nerves were dulled by the heat and support of the water. It felt like she had no body. No body, she thought, as if she were dead—that was what she was doing, getting rid of her body before her body could get rid of her.

Then it came to her: What's the difference? Whether she got rid of her body animal or it got rid of her, it's the same result. The body animal wins. What's the use? Sylvia realized that this body animal would always win, no matter how hard she tried to remain on her mind plane. In the end, her body animal would die. It didn't matter how high and lofty her thoughts. She could develop a cure for cancer, negotiate world peace, and invent a better way to peel an apple—it didn't matter. In the end, her body would take over. This recognition felt like an original thought, like no one else in the world had ever realized this before. She wanted to scream her despair to the people. She couldn't understand how everyone could just go about their business—get up in the morning, shower, go to work, come home, cook dinner, make love, go to sleep. She slid all the way under the water and stayed there as long as she could. Then she sat up, took a deep breath, and pulled the plug. Still sopping wet, she lay on the bed.

How did other people do it? They were whole, integrated—
she was in two parts. Was it possible to un-know something so
fundamental? She didn't think so. She shivered in the cold bed.

Revelations

And the devil, who deceived them, was thrown into the lake of burning sulfur, where the beast and the false prophet had been thrown. They will be tormented day and night for ever and ever. Revelations 20:10

AN, KILLER, AND I are in the Kum & Go snagging some breakfast before heading off to roustabout on the Shoshone oil field. My name's Jimmy, Jimmy Shalinsky, but most people call me Clit. I got the name because I'm good with the ladies. You know, smooth. Dan may have the looks, and Killer may have the size, but I got the talk. I always was a little on the small side, wiry though. Tough, you know— but I can make it with the ladies.

Killer is putting together some nachos. He mounds the chips, ladles hot nacho cheese, and then uses the tongs to try to fish out some jalapenos, but he gets tired of it so he grabs them with his fingers and plops them on top. Then he slurps his fingers.

Dan appraises the bowl and says, "I think you can fit some more on there."

Killer looks at the bowl and then at Dan and grins. "Fire in the hole," Killer says.

"I'll show you fire in the hole," Dan says, glancing over at the fat lady with the gigantic tits behind the counter.

They always have been a pair. They played football at Last Chance High School and took us to the Wyoming state finals in Division 4A. Dan was the quarterback, of course, and Killer was a lineman. Dan really knew how to motivate the team, so I heard—I was a couple of years behind them—and Killer was just that, a killer on the line. They say he broke both legs of this guy from Torrington. The people from Torrington got all hot and bothered because they said it was a dirty hit—he was nowhere near the ball, they said—but the ref didn't see it, so, hey, it might as well not've happened.

Dan's still good looking, just like he was in high school. Fit. Blonde hair that makes him look like a surfer. You wouldn't think he was almost thirty. I don't know how he does it—his clothes are always neat and clean, even when we're working a rig. Killer, though, has let himself go. He has this red beard that bushes out above his considerable gut, and he shaves his head but then wears one of the black Nazi hats with the gold braid on the brim and the eagle on the top.

I take my twenty-ounce coffee to the counter to pay. The fat lady taps the register keys with her cocaine nails and says, "A little go juice?" She's got a ring on her finger, and I wonder what ugly bastard would marry her.

"Yeah—I mean, no," I say, pushing my glasses up my nose. "What I mean is, I don't need no go juice. I'm all go." I count out two dollar bills and flip them on the counter.

"A runt like you?" Big Tits eyes me up and down.

"Ain't no correlation," I say. "Some guys got third legs, you know."

She fingers coins out of the drawer and drops them on the counter in front of me. Two pennies roll off and away.

I don't move to get them.

"Little shits like you are all hat and no cattle," she says, "and I've had more than my share of no cattle." She turns like she's got something to do.

I don't know quite what to say, and just as I'm coming up with something, Dan and Killer come up to the counter. In addition to nachos, Killer's got a sausage with mustard and catsup and a cup of coffee. Dan has a bottle of water.

Dan smiles at Big Tits as he lays a twenty on the counter for Killer's food. "The lady ain't interested in what you're selling, Clit."

"She would be if she knew what she's missing." I try to make it sound all happy, like an invitation instead of the lame comeback it is.

Big Tits smiles at Dan. "Ain't you Dan McCoy?" she asks. He nods and slaps her with what I call his knock-em-dead, a smile that would make the avenging angel himself offer him Lifesavers. Then she launches into this long thing about her dad taking her to all his football games. "My dad was a huge fan," she says.

"That's great," Dan says. "So, what's your name?"

"I'm Betsy, but everyone calls me Bet."

"That's sure a pretty name, Bet."

She smiles as she gives Dan his change.

153

Dan nods just a little as he glances at her hands—he's thought of something. "You know what, Bet? We're having a party later, a kegger. Want to come?"

First I'm hearing of it, but that don't mean anything.

Her eyes widen and then narrow. She looks at Dan without saying anything.

"Don't be like that. There's a bunch of us—some people your age, too, I think. What are you? Twenty?" Dan plays it well, as he always does. She's probably at least twenty-two, and he doesn't insult her by saying she's eighteen because when you're young you always want to be older, but she probably just starting to want to be flattered as younger, so he runs it down the middle.

"Well, I'm married," Big Tits says, holding her left hand and splaying out her fingers to show her ring. Then her fleshy shoulders pop up and down, but her eyes stay fixed on his face.

Killer's standing there. He grunts and takes his food and goes out to the truck.

Dan leans forward with his elbows on the counter. He lowers his voice to a growly whisper. "Well, pretty Bet, don't you deserve a night out with the girls?"

Her smile tips up at the corners.

Dan continues, "You just tell your husband you need a night out. What he don't know, won't hurt him."

She shakes her head. "Tom—that's my husband—ain't too keen on me going out." She hesitates and there's silence as she considers, but then her shoulders relax. "But I have my ways to convince him." She leans forward too, her face cutting into the usual comfort distance between two people.

I wonder whether she'll play the bitch card or she'll have sex with her husband to put him in a good mood. Then I get an image of those huge tits flopping up and down and up and down and my dick perks up.

Dan's smile goes from dazzling to fixed—he's gotten what he wants, and so he loses interest in her. "You tell your dad that Dan McCoy says hi," he says as we turn to leave.

"I get off at seven," she says, her head craning around the tall jerky jar.

Dan doesn't reply. We head out to the Dan's brand new duely. It's fire-engine red with a shiny roll-bar and growl pipes. In the gun rack, Dan keeps what he calls his fuck-stick—just hefty and long enough to fuck some bastard up—and a twenty-two semi-auto for hunting coyotes.

Sitting on the open tailgate is Killer, and he's got his hand out to a magpie perched on the side. The bird's black-and-white-tuxedoed body poses then jerks as it eyes Killer and then pecks at his fingers. Killer's small pig eyes are round and open. When he sees us, he pulls back his hand and his face closes in. The bird launches into the air. Killer pushes himself off the tailgate and grabs his nachos.

"Looks like Adam's in the garden," Dan says as he walks past him.

Killer doesn't say anything. He walks around to my side. As I'm climbing into the cab, he says, "Clit calls the bitch seat." What he always says every time.

"Better a bitch than a fucking asshole." What I say every time. *Gayboy*, I add silently.

Dan and Killer get in. Dan starts the engine and the radio blares. It's the news. I reach to turn it down and Dan slaps my hand. "Leave it." He shifts, backs out, and rods it onto the street while a woman with a deep monotone reports a one car rollover that killed a husband and wife from Colorado and that the rig count is up. Then the program switches to a slow-talking cattle report.

I glance over at Killer and he's looking past me at Dan. Killer shakes his head.

Dan looks at Killer from the corner of his eye and says, "They don't report, uh, overenthusiastic sex. Due to the sensitive nature of the subject." He flashes a smile that doesn't reach his eyes.

"Lucky for me," Killer says.

"Besides, it's old news by now," Dan says.

"What're you guys talking about?" I say.

"Mind your own," Killer says in a deep voice.

So I do.

We're in the second week of our two weeks on. Twelve-hour days. Mostly we work our asses off moving equipment and supplies, cleaning up garbage and spills, painting—shit like that. It stinks to high heaven, and grit gets into my every crack and cranny. If my fingers ain't black from oil, they're black from getting whacked. Sometimes it's so hot you could fry an egg. Sometimes it snows so hard it's all you can do to keep your balls from freezing. Dan's almost charmed his way from roustabout to roughneck, and he'll take Killer with him. I'm hoping he takes me along too.

It's before seven, so we've got time to make it from Last Chance to the pad before our shift starts. The blacktop skirts along the wide shallow reaches of the Big Sulfur—named for the hotsprings that feeds into it—and in and out of stands of

156

cottonwoods and fields of sugar beets and alfalfa. This time of year, the vegetation's turned from bright green to deep green, and soon it'll be shading to brown where it's not irrigated. Or everywhere if we have the drought like last year. Dan downshifts and turns onto the gravel county road. We thread up a ravine and onto the dry sagebrush benches that line the river valley. The air changes. You can feel it coming through Dan's cracked window—what was cool and moist turns hot, pungent, and dusty. The radio says it'll get up to a hundred and three. The patchy sagebrush is interspersed with sand dunes. The drought's killed off enough of the vegetation that the wind scoops sand out of one place and deposits it in another. It's like the earth's trying reclaim the whole countryside.

"Maybe next year, they'll hire us on as roughnecks," I say with an eye toward Dan. "That way, I can buy my own transportation, not have to hitch with you." Can't hurt to give Dan a little more incentive. What I really want is to save up enough to get my mama into one of those programs where they dry out. It don't work to have her in A.A. She just gets tanked before she attends the meetings till they kick her out.

"Skinny shit like you? No fucking way," Killer says as he pushes in the cigarette lighter. He pokes his finger and thumb into his pack of cigarettes and fishes one out, zips the window down, and when the lighter pops he presses the glowing rings to the tip of his cigarette and sucks in the air. Then he sticks the lighter back into the ashtray.

"Don't worry about it," Dan says. "World's going to end this year."

"What?" I say.

157

"Yeah, those crackpots are saying 2010's the end of the world."

I don't like telling Dan he's wrong, but I say, "That's 2012. The end of the Mayan calendar." My mama digs things like that, so I know.

"Well, I'm saying it's 2010." He lets out a burst of air.

I shrug.

We pop up over a hill, the gravel crunching under our tires, and two deer, does, stand broadside in the middle of the road. Dan stamps down on the brakes and the truck slides to a halt. Billowing dust engulfs us from behind and veils the sun. The doe in front stumbles forward and then high-steps off the gravel. Once she reaches the borrow ditch, she bounds across the unmown grass and leaps the barbed wire fence on Dan's side of the truck. The other smaller doe continues to stand broadside looking at us, like she can't quite figure out what we are.

I glance at Dan and Killer. Dan's head is cocked to one side, but Killer's eyes have opened up again and he's leaning forward, his beard detached from his chest. Dan turns off the radio. Then he twists sideways toward me, his arms reaching over my left shoulder, and I lean forward to give him room. He's pulling the twenty-two out of the gun rack.

"Hey, Killer," Dan says, "ever had venison backstrap?"

"Yeah," is all Killer says. He ducks as Dan tips the rifle over our heads and points the muzzle to the floorboards.

"What do you think?"

"We're going to be late," Killer says. I'm sure he knows how lame this sounds.

"A clean kill, and we can be in and out in five minutes," Dan says. He lifts the rifle across my lap toward Killer.

"We don't need no backstrap."

"Ah, come on, Killer."

"Dan, we don't need no venison."

"Sure we do."

"Well, if we need it so goddamn bad, you shoot it." Killer's face is turning red. He's always had a quick temper. I lean away from him toward Dan.

"You're the killer, *Killer*. What's the matter? You chickenshit?"

"I ain't chickenshit."

"Bwock, bwock, bwo-ock," Dan says. Holding the stock with his left hand, he reaches past me with his right and slaps Killer on the chest with his palm.

"He don't want to shoot it," I say.

"Shut the fuck up," Killer says to me. He says to Dan, "You want me to fucking poach a deer?"

"Killer's decided to go all Greenie treehugger on us, Clit. He's a sensitive new-age guy."

Killer doesn't say anything for a minute, and Dan doesn't either, just leans forward holding the gun and staring at Killer.

Eyes on the dash, Killer moves his head back and forth slightly. "Just give me the gun," Killer says. Dan smiles, showing his teeth, and hands the gun to Killer. Killer takes it, pushes open the door, steps to the hood, chambers a round, and leans forward, propping the stock to his shoulder and his elbows on the hood.

The bigger doe is long gone, but the smaller one is in the borrow ditch bounding back and forth along the fenceline trying to get up the courage to jump. Killer doesn't wait for her to stop. One report, then two more in quick succession. The doe leaps like a rabbit and then falls down onto her front knees and collapses forward then onto her side, her head bent back over her shoulder.

Dan pulls open the glove box and retrieves a big Buck knife. He pushes open the door and gets out, glances both ways down the road, and then walks quickly over to the kicking doe. I stay in the truck. Killer doesn't even glance Dan's way. He clears the cartridge and uses his thumb to keep the next round from entering the chamber. He comes back to the cab. He's careful as he lifts the gun over my head and places it back in the rack. He gets in and shuts the door. Dan's over at the animal. He doesn't bleed her out or anything. He just slices through the hide on the back, peels it away, and then cuts along the backbone and ribs on each side to remove the backstrap, laying the first one on the grass while he cuts the second. He flips the knife shut, picks up the meat, and comes to the truck. He opens an empty gunny sack on the tailgate and wraps up the meat and tucks it up next to the cab. He wipes his hands on his jeans and then comes up and gets in the truck.

"We'll start a fire out at the pad," he says. "Roast them for lunch." He starts the truck, glances in his rearview, and then peels out, his bloody palm twirling the steering wheel and his head bobbing like he's listening to his own inner music. Killer just stares forward.

We spend the morning cleaning up the pad. That's our job for the day. Our boss—his name is Rick but we call him Rick the Dick—told us to do what's necessary. He thinks the inspectors'll be out next week. We pick up the sandwich wrappers and soda cans. We slop paint over rusty metal. We dump empty fifty-five gallon drums all into one big pile. We smooth out places where oil has spilled and cover them over with more dirt and sand from the reserve pile—they shouldn't soak through till after the inspectors have come and gone.

Late in the morning while Killer rolls drums and I slop paint, Dan gathers dead sagebrush limbs and some larger pieces of driftwood washed by spring storms into the gully that skirts the pad. He starts a fire. Then he continues to work but stops every once in a while to pile wood on the fire, so that it all burns down to orange and white coals. Around noon, he pours water over the backstraps and lays them over the bed of coals. Soon the smell of cooking meat makes my stomach growl.

"You bastards ready to eat?" Dan says.

Killer and I go over to the tailgate where he's cutting off chunks of meat. We stand around and eat with our fingers. It's a bit gritty, but the char of the sagebrush adds to the flavor. Killer seems to have forgotten where the meat came from, as he doesn't even hesitate. Between the three of us, we polish off both hunks. Killer sits down on the tailgate and licks his fingers.

"This is the best venison I've ever had," I say to no one in particular.

"Clit's a venison virgin?" Dan says with a buggy look on his face.

I have to think for a minute. Then I say, "No, I said it was the best, not the first."

"Yeah? So Clit's had venison, but has he had a woman?"

"I'm thinking not," Killer says.

"I have too," I say. It's none of their fucking business if I have or haven't.

"So Clit's not only a virgin, but he's a liar," Dan says.

"You guys are so full of shit," I say.

"Admit it," Dan says and takes a step toward me. "Come on, say 'I'm a lying virgin.' Come on, say it."

I take a step backwards. Killer hops down from where he's sitting on the tailgate.

"Say it, Clit," Dan says. "'I'm a lying virgin.'" He takes another step toward me and Killer walks up beside him.

There's no way I'm going to say it. No fucking way. But Dan's gone squirrely and Killer's backing him up—they're not going to stop until they make me say it. I've seen it before—they're like a couple of wild dogs once they fix on something.

I glance through the back window at the rifle, but I can't get to the front of the truck, jerk open the door, pull out the rifle, and jack a shell before they're on me. I glance around.

"Say it," Dan says. "Say it." He and Killer are walking forward and I'm stepping backwards.

"You're going to fucking say it," Dan says.

I turn and take off running. I don't look back—I know they're right behind me. Killer's enough out of shape I'm not worried about him, but Dan's got stick and the stamina to back it up.

Ahead of me I see the fire, and poking up from it is a good-sized branch. As I run past, I lean down and snag it and then take a quick jog right. Then I spin and huck it hard as I can at Dan's head. Dan ducks sideways and the branch sails past him. I turn to run but then Dan's on me. I trip and land on my face and he's on my back grabbing for my arms. It knocks the wind out of me and my glasses go flying, but I'm struggling to keep my arms free and pushing against the ground, trying to get to my hands and knees. He manages to wrench my left arm behind me and up to my shoulder blade. The pain shoots through it and into my shoulder. I try to twist sideways to release the pressure, but his weight on my butt keeps me pinned.

"You're nothing but empty talk, Jimmy," Dan says, "and the only woman you've had is your drunk-ass mother."

"Fuck you," I say and jerk hard as I can.

"You're a worthless piece of shit. I want you to say it. Say it, you fuckhead."

I'm not going to say it. There's no way I'm going to say it. If I say it, they'll let me go, sure. Yesterday, I would've. But not today. Today, my mama made me eggs for breakfast. She got herself out of bed and made me eggs. That ought to be worth something.

My arm is released, and I think, okay, but then his grip wraps around my throat. His hands are warm and moist and the pads of his fingers dig into the soft parts of my neck. My adam's apple jams flat. I have to cough but I can't. At first it's like when you hold your breath. Not too bad. I pull my arm from my back, try to push myself up. Dan's weight's in the middle of my back, though, can't do a pushup with that monkey on my back. He rattles me, and my head snaps back and forward, back and forward. There, a smidgen of breath, but then he clamps down again. My lungs strain, try to pull in air. My heart thumps, thumps, thumps. Try to muscle it and then wildly squirm and push. Almost. He's leaning forward and I knock him off balance, my body halfway out from under. But air, air, air. Fwoop, the senses shut down.

Nothing.

"You kill him?" It's Killer's voice coming from above and to the left.

My throat. It hurts. I cough. I cough again.

There's silence.

I push myself onto my back. My arms ache and my neck and my back where I twisted it. I crack open my eyes but it's so bright. I slam them shut and pull my arm over my face. My glasses are gone.

Killer: "You fucking lost it, man." His voice is more urgent, higher, than I've ever heard it.

Dan: "Shut up." He's to my right.

Killer: "I've never seen you that pissed off."

Dan: "Just shut the fuck up."

Killer: "No, you really lost it. You were going to kill him."

I feel Dan loom over me and I curl to protect my stomach, but he doesn't touch me and instead I hear the scuffle of dirt as Killer steps back.

"You let that piss-ant get to you," Killer says softly.

Dan steps over me and I hear an *oomph*. I crack my eyes in time to see Killer on his ass in the dirt and Dan standing over him.

This has never happened before. Something's been broke. Killer's always been the hands to Dan's body.

From beyond us, there's a distinct *whooomp!* I don't know what it is. I hear Dan say, "Shit," and then after a bit he and then Killer walk over toward the sound.

I carefully stretch to see if I've busted anything. Don't seem to. I cautiously push myself up and teeter to my feet. I don't even look for my glasses—I can see how it is well enough without them. I walk up behind Dan and Killer but keep my distance. Dan's shoulders are back, his head cocked. Killer's off to one side and hunkered a bit, his arm across his stomach.

They're standing in front of the pile of barrels, which is engulfed in flame. The flames aren't just orange. They flare up in patches of blue and then green. They flick and weave. We stand and watch, but the heat rises and soon we're forced to take a step back. The flames continue to climb higher, straighter now, more frantic, grasping up to heaven like the northern lights.

Then, a weird thing. The barrels start to bulge. The sides warp and round outwards. There's a creaking, metal stress. I have a split second to think, *get the fuck out of here*, and then the whole thing explodes. I see flames engulf Dan and Killer and then they're on me. I'm surrounded by flames, I feel the pressure of their blast, but there's nothing, no pain. I marvel at this. I back away, and still the flames cocoon me. It feels like all the air's been sucked away—I can't breathe, I pull and pull but there's no air, my shirt is burning and my pants are burning and the acrid odor of burned hair reaches my nostrils and something else, like cooked venison, I glance down, my right hand is black but still in the shape of a hand, large pieces of skin hang from my left hand, I wonder what my face looks like, I should be in pain, but I don't feel anything, I think, *you know what, I'm going to die, yep, that's it, it's the end* people don't survive something like this wait that fireman who lived but then nobody could look at him not just because his flesh was shapeless like a potato but because he carried himself all stiff and twisted like the flames deformed his insides that house fire in Last Chance where the kid burned to death I'm waiting for the pain to come what happened to his mama? no pain what does that mean? the flames surround me I'm the kid not the fireman fall to knees we're all gonna

Dammed

THE OLD MAN'S FACE WAS WRINKLED AND BROWN and caved in like a wintered-over apple. It didn't matter that he was wearing his teeth. His bad eye, filmed over with white, he kept wide open, while he squinted with his good right eye, which was deep brown and took in everything. He craned his neck as he steered the old irrigation truck down the wheel ruts, his broad hands gripping either side of the wheel.

"I can respect a woman who gets money for it," he told the girl without looking at her. "A woman who just does it cause she wants to, she's a slut." His voice took on an eager quality as he said this.

The girl, who was only 12 but tall and strong for her age, tried to soak in this new information. What did it mean, exactly? She knew from TV that it was okay for boys who were older, for men, to want it and to get it. In fact, if they didn't want it and go after the girls, they were thought of as abnormal, not quite right, and there were whispers that these boys did *things*. But girls weren't supposed want it. That's what the old man said. It was okay if girls did it as a job, perfectly all right, but if they wanted it in the same way boys wanted it, there was something horribly wrong akin to those boys who didn't want girls at all.

It didn't make sense, but there it was.

Later, long after the old man had died and she was grown, the girl would wonder what prompted the old man to say it. She couldn't remember what they had been talking about before. Probably he had been telling a story about some woman in town. He had loved to gossip, and she could still picture his small eager frame as he laid out details over the kitchen table to her mother. Or had it been something about her that had made him say it?

IT WAS THE GIRL'S JOB THAT SUMMER to go with the old man, the hired hand, who wasn't quite as spry as he used to be, that's what her dad said, and help irrigate the fields of mostly alfalfa, with some sugar beets and corn. Irrigation, or changing water, was the job you did to make things grow, and there were four sets of water to be changed every morning and every afternoon. They would drive the two-track roads that wound around the creek and through hills and the fields, the old man gunning the motor through the boggy places. The girl loved the feeling of acceleration down the hill, her body pressed back against the cracked vinyl seat, the air rushing in the window, and then her body thrown forward as *splash* they hit the water-filled dip at the bottom and the muddy water spraying out and blocking her view all around the truck and the fine mist coming in through the window cool against her skin.

When they reached the field with its scraggly patches of young plants, the girl would reach through the open window to the outside and yank the handle up and put her weight into the door so that it opened with a screechy groaning. She would retrieve her shovel and, if needed, the extra orange plastic-canvas dam with its almost-straight cottonwood bough as a support threaded through the tarp's sleeve. In her thigh-high rubber waders, she followed the old man as he, shovel propped military style on his shoulder, bow-leggedly whistled his way across the hills or along the ditch bank. As they walked, the old man smoothly negotiated sandy drop-offs and picked his way through cactus patches and, every once in a while, held up his hand to stop her so that a rattlesnake sunning itself under a bush could sidle its way into the sagebrush, tongue flicking and head weaving to catch scent.

The girl loved the sounds. The tinkle of the water over a rock lodged in the ditch. The soft fwump-fwump of their rubber boots against the packed earth of the deer path. The decisive slice of the shovel as it bit into the moist ditch bank. The cheerful meandering call of the meadowlark with its three quick notes like leaping upstairs at the end.

Once they made it to the set, the old man's eyes would sweep out over the watery field, focusing on one part while skimming over another. "That there is good and soaked," he would sometimes say. Or he might say, "Well, I'll be pocket gopher, would you look at that?" Not even glancing her direction, he would point toward the field, and the longer she was around him the more she knew what he meant by slight differences in intonation. Sometimes it was a coyote head-down and loping up the ridge slope or a herd of tawny white-tails making their way through the old apple orchard and once it was a mountain lion panting in the shade of a tall juniper bush. But usually it was the water that had done something unexpected—cut across three rows and totally missed a spot or spread to cover an area that he'd thought would be missed. If he wasn't happy, he'd say, "Well, I'll be god-damned," or "Useless as tits on a boar," and he'd shake his head.

To change the set, the girl would yank out one side of the horizontal support pole, which let the three vertical supports fall away, and the pressure of the water would pull the dam from its tampings and the water would come rushing under it like a bull through a matador's cape. If she couldn't budge the support pole, she'd try to work out one of the three vertical stick braces that rested against the long horizontal one. If they all were stuck tight, which they usually were, she'd work at the upstream end of the orange plastic-canvas, pulling it from where it had been tamped in by the shovel, dislodging clods that had held it in place, and letting the water flow past and relieving the pressure.

The old man would stand back, his head thrust forward as he watched, his eyes silently commenting. He wasn't strong anymore and short of breath from smoking, so over time they'd come to understand that it was just better if she worked at it by herself, even if she was clumsy.

The girl would then flop the muddy tarp open on the bank and put the support pole and the brace sticks into the orange plastic-canvas and roll it together as tightly as she could. The old man would pick up her shovel and prop it on his shoulder next to his and she would wrap her arms around the wet awkward bundle, soaking her shirtsleeves and often her belly, and they would walk down the ditch aways until the old man stopped and nodded. The girl would drop the dam and unroll it and retrieve the pole. She would lay it perpendicular to the ditch downstream of the slight notch made last year or five years ago that let water out into the small feeder ditch, which was nothing more than a slight dip trailing along the outside of the main ditch to help spread water. She would try to wedge the pole against hummocks. Then she would angle the three braces at at least 45 degrees as she poked them into the water and mud and laid them back against the pole. Finally, she placed the support pole of the dam in front of the pole and braces. She stepped back and, with her arms held wide like wings, she held each upstream corner of the plastic-canvas hovering over the water.

This was the moment the girl savored. One swift movement decided whether she'd done the job. Later, she would get the same feeling in high school before a date and in college before an exam and the morning of her wedding day and just after her husband asked her for a divorce. It was a feeling of possibility, of diversion, of escape. Sometimes she would worry that she was addicted to the feeling, that she changed her life too much because it had been running along the same ditch too long, that she never let it set long enough to let anything grow. She would wonder if there was a moment she could have changed things, she could have set her dam, or not set her dam, and her life would have been profoundly different. But most of the time she didn't think about it.

Holding the corners up, the girl would let the middle sag and then step on it with her rubber-booted foot to force it below the water. Then she bent forward and splayed out her arms as if she were holding the corners of a skirt in order to curtsey and laid the corners of the dam as close to the banks as possible. The water quickly caught, and it ballooned like a sail against the supports. At this point, the girl had only a spare second to make sure the canvas laid down right before the weight of the water pinned it in place. If it wasn't right, the whole set had to be pulled and placed again. But it didn't take long before her actions were smooth and sure and resulted in the quick bulge of canvas against the wood.

She loved the cool of the water through her boots and on her leg. The first time she had tried out her new irrigation boots—which had the rubber tire smell of the Big R Farm and Ranch Supply where they'd bought them—she'd stepped in the water and immediately thought that the boots were defective and her feet and legs were soaked, but when she stepped out, they were warm and dry. So she stepped in, and again her feet felt wet. Then she stepped in and out and in and out, just so she could feel the water's deception against her skin.

If the dam was well-set, the water mounted against the plastic until it was high enough to creep and then rush out the notch in the bank and spread down in the feeder ditch and into the field. As the girl tamped the dam into place and scooped shovelfuls of dirt to secure it, the old man shepherded the water out across the field. He would deftly direct the water by scooping shallow trenches and laying efficient rows of clods. In one smooth motion, he could prop his shovel tip into the bank, stomp down with his foot to dislodge a clump, scoop it up, and toss it to the exact spot necessary to divert the water where it needed to go. He hummed as he did all this.

Once he was done, the old man would survey the field again and watch as the leading edge of the water crept down the rows. The girl could tell when he was satisfied because he would prop the shovel against his shoulder, fish in his pocket, and pull out the wallet-like packet of Prince Albert tobacco and rolling papers and a book of matches. He would deftly hold the paper in one hand, sprinkle the tobacco with the other, lick the edge, and then seal it. The cigarette might look misshapen, especially later when it hung half burned and half-forgotten from the old man's lip, but the girl knew that it was tight. The old man would then tuck the packet away, flick a paper match against its striker, and inhale deeply as he lit the cigarette. He always held his breath after that first inhale and then let it out in a long sigh.

BUT TODAY THEY WERE GETTING AN EARLY START because it was going to be a long day. Instead of coming back to the house at noon, they'd each packed a lunch. First they'd change water and then they would drive the long windy two-track that skirted along the bench to the main dam in the creek that fed the long series of ditches. The water had started to erode around it, and it was their job to fix it as best they could until they could borrow the neighbors' backhoe and drive it the long miles up to the dam and reinforce it with dirt and boulders. The girl had her swimsuit on under her clothes because she knew she'd be the one in the water. Once they'd fixed the dam, it was back to change the sets again.

As they wound their way toward the first set, the girl thought about *it*. For a couple of years now, the girl's body had been having special yearnings, which had been getting stronger as she got older. She had first noticed it when she had seen their dog Gilly mounted by the neighbor dog. It had made her feel both squirmy and relaxed at the same time. She had wanted something, but she didn't know what. She had settled for stealing a sliver of lemon cake with sugary sweet icing from the refrigerator and shoveling it quickly into her mouth before her mom came into the kitchen. Then, during the summer, a city cousin had visited and stayed in her room, while she had been moved to the couch on the back screen porch. After he left, she discovered that he had dropped a paperback between the bed and the wall. The book was called *Hollywood Horny* and had the stylized image on the front of a movie actress winking over her sunglasses. Her nipples made distinct bumps in the blue cloth of her low-cut shirt. The book described men and women doing things that the girl had not thought possible. Some of the things disgusted her, but some of them made her tingly all over, and it was then that she discovered that she could tickle her arms and her breasts to enhance the feeling. Soon she began imagining a dark man coming through her bedroom door. She could see his bare muscled chest but not his face. Then she began touching herself between her legs and it immediately sent a shock wave through her and she convulsed and it felt good, and she thought, ah, this is what the book is about. She began to do it regularly and hid the book.

But now, sitting in the cab of the truck as it lurched over the ruts, the girl realized that what she had been doing was wrong. She had suspected it before now, but now that it had been verbalized it came almost as an epiphany, and she felt herself blush all over. It was not only wrong, it was akin to what those unnatural boys did. Her body clenched in shame, and she fixed her gaze out the window. Her body had betrayed her in some deep and fundamental way, she realized now.

As they changed the first and second set, the girl focused on the motions of work and did not let her mind wander. As the old man drove to their third set, there came the shiny blue truck of their neighbors to the south, newlyweds who were expecting their first child. Rather than sitting next to the passenger window, the woman had scooted to the middle, despite her large belly, and she sat right next to the man.

The old man pulled off to the side of the road and held up his palm as the couple pulled up and stopped. The young man rolled down his window and said, "Heya," as the woman leaned forward to peek past her husband. The woman raised a hand and gave a parade wave, her cupped palm rotating back and forth.

"Neighbor," the old man said.

The young man nodded toward the old man and then glanced toward his wife.

"Spring's coming on fine this year," the old man said.

"Yes," the young man said.

"Good year for a garden."

The young man took a deep breath, let it out, and then said, "Yes." Then he bowed his head quickly toward his wife and said something to her and then turned back. "Alfalfa's coming up good," he added.

"Yeah," said the old man. "Amazing what a little water will do."

There was silence between them. The old man didn't say anything but didn't seem ready to end the conversation.

The young man shook his head and then said, without much expression in his voice, "So, any chance we can open that headgate a bit? The wife keeps pestering me about getting those greenhouse starts into the ground."

The couple's greenhouse was next to their house but their garden was way up near an apple orchard, far enough that it couldn't be watered by the hose. Their ditch to the garden was fed by the same headgate as the girl's family's fields—a headgate that was padlocked, and the old man had the key. The girl had seen the young man out there with the rototiller almost two weeks ago preparing the ground to plant. The brown patch had lain undisturbed since.

"Say," said the old man, his voice eager, "weren't there one of those sleek sedans parked out at your place the other day? Or was it one of those rich-rancher trucks?"

"Might've been," the young man said and played with the mirror on his door, adjusting it forward and then back.

"That was about the time you went back to—where was it?—Kansas? Iowa? One of them conferences, wasn't it?"

The man didn't answer.

"Relatives in town?" the old man said.

The young man looked hard at the old man. "You know very well that that was my mother-in-law up from Arizona. And I don't like what—" The young man stopped short as he turned to his wife and said something. He turned back. "Anyway, it was my mother-in-law getting things ready for when the baby comes."

The old man nodded and chuckled. "Yeah, when the mother-in-law visits, it's best to clear out of town. There are some things you just don't want to be around for." Then, as if it was his idea, he said, "Say, didn't you need water for your garden?"

The young man didn't say anything, just looked at him.

"Tomorrow first thing, sevenish," the old man said, "meet me at the headgate."

"Thank you," the wife said past her husband. "He'll be there."

As soon as the couple pulled away, the old man laughed. "He'll be thinking about that for weeks. Them rich ranchers." He laughed again.

The girl didn't understand exactly what had happened, but she understood that he'd gotten to the young man somehow. The old man had loved it, whatever it was.

It didn't seem right, though, that the couple had had to wait to put in their garden. They were such a beautiful young couple. She had seen them in town walking down the street together, laughing, back before they were married, and she had once caught a glimpse of them kissing on the porch before the young man drove off to his job at the co-op in town. She had kept that image close to her—the way the man had stepped down a tier on the front steps so that his wife would not have to stand on tiptoe. How he'd leaned forward at first, his elbows poked out behind him, but then when his wife had wrapped her arms around his neck he had put his arms around her waist and pulled her to him. It seemed, for a second, they had melded into one being. It had made the girl feel something like when she stroked her own arms, only it wasn't so much in the body as in the very center of her.

Had her parents once been like this young couple? The girl couldn't imagine it.

In high school, her mother had been both valedictorian and head cheerleader. Her mother had shown the girl all four of her high school yearbooks. It seemed that her mother was on every page. Here her brown hair, long back then, is in pigtails and she's dressed in bib overalls and bobby socks for a production of *Our Town*. There she stands at the center of a group of five girls in matching dresses with scalloped collars, their mouths in *O*s and their necks craned as they sing. Here she sits in a booth opposite a boy, and they both lean forward sipping straws from the same soda fountain glass. The caption reads, "Our very own golden couple doing their best Norman Rockwell." The boy is not the girl's father, and this bothers the girl whenever she sees that photo. The fact that her parents had not always been together, that maybe there had been others in the past, made her think that maybe there could be others in the future, no matter how stable her parents' marriage seemed. And it wasn't just this photo. Sometimes her mother would be washing dishes and staring off into space. It would make the girl so uncomfortable she would find an excuse to draw her mother's attention. Once, when the girl had woken up in the middle of the night and had to go to the bathroom, a flickering of light from down the hall drew her. It was her mother sitting on the living room couch surrounded by her yearbooks and other things with just a flashlight for light.

The girl's father had grown up on this farm. Her small bedroom, with its dark-paneled walls, had been his boyhood bedroom. Her father had gone to the same high school as her mother, only six years before her. Snooping in her parent's bedroom, the girl could only find one of his yearbooks, the one from his senior year. In it, there were only two photos of him—his senior portrait and one with his head peeking just over the shoulder of another boy in a group of Future Farmers of

America. The senior portrait was not really a senior portrait at all but a snapshot of him in a plaid western shirt standing in front of some bushes and smiling uncomfortably, as if he was at a backyard barbecue and someone had just said something that he thought was funny but also slightly embarrassing.

In the albums, there were only a few photos of her parents when they were courting. There was one where they stood on opposite ends of a church group and another where they stood arm-in-arm in deep snow by the door of a car. There was only one on the day they got married. It was slightly blurry, as if the photographer had been in a hurry and shook the camera. The expression on her mother's face was a little fixed, as if she'd smiled the moment before and then had to keep smiling as she waited for the photographer to push the button. On her father's face was a genuine smile but his eyes were wide as if he were a little bit frightened.

Now, thinking about the young neighbor couple, the girl tried to think of a time when she had seen her parents touch. She certainly had never seen them kiss or hug, but she couldn't even think of her father's hand on her mother's arm or their shoulders accidentally brushing. When they sat together in the car or on the couch, the girl always sat between them, and they had let her sleep in their bed until she had mentioned it at school and the other kids had teased her about it and she had decided to sleep in her own bed.

THE OLD MAN AND THE GIRL CHANGED THE LAST TWO SETS and then drove the long jouncy way around the backside of the hills and across the canyon and up through the bushes taller than the truck and over the dry beds of draws to where the tracks of the road were no more than faint traces grown over with weeds. It was noon by the time they reached the shade of a group of cottonwoods near where the dam diverted the water down the main canal that led to the various head gates.

The old man let the truck coast to a stop in the shade and then turned off the key. Without the breeze in through the window of the truck, the cab quickly became so warm that sweat began seeping from the undersides of the girls leg's and down her ribs. The old man sat for a couple seconds before he turned to the girl, nodded toward her metal lunch box on the floor, and then picked his lunch off the seat next to him. His lunch, a kitchen towel with its opposite corners knotted together, was two burritos of pork and beans and wieners rolled in flour tortillas and fried in bacon grease. When the old man opened the towel, the smell drifted through the cab and made the girl's mouth water. The girl opened her box. Her mother had packed an old orange juice bottle full of cow's milk, a hunk of cheese, and two leftover pancakes spread with peanut butter and honey and rolled.

They ate. The girl propped her milk bottle between her legs as she ate bites of rolled pancake and licked the dripping honey from the bottom of the pancake and from her fingers. Then she ate the cheese the way she liked to. Instead of big bites, she liked to nibble little bits and savor them and to take big drinks of milk between each bite. She almost always ran out of milk before she ran out of cheese. When that happened, she put the cheese away and didn't eat the rest of it, no matter how hungry she was.

Just as the girl was stowing her milk bottle and the last small bit of cheese in her lunch box, the old man choked. He began gagging and coughing and his false teeth clacked together as he tried to clear the obstruction from his throat. The girl didn't know quite what to do, but the old man held out his hand and shook his head as he was coughing, indicating she shouldn't do anything. It was excruciating, listening to the old man gagging and trying to draw breath. After what seemed like a long time, he finally got it under control.

The girl asked, "Are you all right?"

The old man breathed for a minute and then wheezed, "Been having trouble swallowing lately. But I'm fine."

She did not know it, of course, but the old man would only live a scant six months more. He would not return from a weekend in town. This was not at all unusual though. Every couple of months, the old man liked to collect his paycheck and go on a bender. He'd show up back at the farm on Monday or Tuesday, his sweat smelling of booze. But it would be a Thursday this time, and the girl would be with her father when he spotted the irrigation truck parked alongside the dingy motel out on the old highway. Her father glanced at her before pulling up behind the truck and parking. "Stay here," was all he said. She watched as he pounded on the door of the room and then tried the knob, which was open. Her father stuck his head in and said something and then, after hesitating a moment, went in. A few minutes passed before her father pushed back out the door, glanced both directions, and then quickstepped to the truck. He pulled open the driver's side door, stashed some magazines and a stick under the driver's seat, and told her, "You'll keep your eyes above the dash, if you know what's good for you." When he went into motel office, of course the girl popped her head down to look. What she saw scared her so badly that she sat back up and stared straight ahead. The stick was a sawed-off broom handle with the end covered with what looked like a deflated balloon, and on the cover of the top magazine were two men standing side by side in nothing but boxer shorts. They were holding hands.

After the old man and the girl had eaten their lunch, they were ready to fix the dam on the creek. They got out of the truck, and the girl kicked off her waders and tossed them into the back. She pulled off her shirt and shorts so she was just in her bathing suit and loosely folded the clothes and put them on the front seat. She retrieved her old sneakers from the cab and put them on and tied them. It felt good to be out of the heavy waders and clothes, with the sweat drying and cooling her skin. The old man gathered both their shovels and the girl picked up the heavy awkward roll of plastic-canvas tarp, deep blue instead of orange, and tried to find a way to carry it. It was too big to rest on her shoulder and she had a hard time wrapping her arms around it. She ended up hooking both arms underneath and raring her body back to compensate for the weight. The ends stuck way out, and she had to walk sideways through the trees, her arms straining against gravity and the inertia of the swinging roll.

They walked down a hillside and through some trees and into the old dry rocky meander of the creek bed. She was so focused on walking over the stones without twisting her ankle while maintaining her balance that she bumped into the old man as he stood in the middle of the creek bed. "STOP," the old man said, his voice a short yip. His hand was up and spread. She swayed to a stop and then stepped back and let one side of the huge roll drop to the ground.

An old eddy of the creek bed was now a spit of dry sand, and it looked like the sand was boiling. The girl focused on it and saw that it was a huge rattlesnake coiled and writhing around itself in intricate knots but with its head pointed toward the sky.

"Is it rabid?" the girl asked. She didn't know if snakes could catch rabies, but she couldn't think of anything else that would cause an animal to act so crazy.

"Shshsh," the old man said. "They're loving."

So there were two rattlesnakes braided together. She could see that now. Both their heads were pointed toward the sky, and they were taking turns weaving into one another's bodies. One's head would reach upwards and then curve toward the other's head and its body would twirl overtop of the other's and then it would fall and dip, and then the other would, creating an intricate dance and weave and rubbing of bodies. Sometimes their heads would twist round and round each other until they fell forward under their own weight. Sometimes both heads would shoot toward the sky and they would rise and fall as one.

Watching this made the girl's body open up to all that it was sensing. Even after the snakes were out of sight and she and the old man skirted a thicket of bushes, the girl felt it. She was in the world, of the world. There it was: the tawny colors of nature illuminated from within, the twee of birds and the steady tinkle of water and the rush of leaves in the breeze, the smell of muddy places and baking dirt and growing things, the heat of the sun on her legs and the cool of the breeze in her hair and the soft scratch of bushes and weighty crinkle of the plastic-canvas against her arms. Even as she and the old man worked to stop the rush of water that was eroding one end of the earthen dike that skirted the concrete spillway, she felt this. Even as they stuck poles into the opening and as they spread plastic-canvas over the top and hefted in rocks to weight the canvas down.

Then the feeling settled into her groin and she felt it feeling rising there. Oh my god, she thought. Oh my god. What had she done? This is wrong, so wrong, what she was feeling. The girl stepped into the deep pool of cold water behind the dam under the pretense of adjusting the blue plastic-canvas, and she let her body sink in the water. She couldn't, shouldn't feel this. This couldn't happen. The cold water sent goose bumps up and down her torso and her arms, it was so cold. She must have a particular weakness for feeling, she thought, and it could come at any time. What could she do? She stepped deeper in and then dipped down and put her head under the water so that all of her was surrounded by frigid water. She must always be on her guard against it. Always. This resistance must become a part of her. She must not feel, she thought, and then the cold water did the trick and she did not feel.

Wanting

Southern Montana, 1908

EMMALINE REMEMBERS THE COLD THAT NIGHT, how her toes were solid and unfeeling in her boots as she stepped off Bob, patted his neck, and handed the reins to Joseph. Water trickled under the ice in the creek, horses' hooves thumped softly in the dry scuff of the corral, and saddle leathers creaked. Just a whiff of wood smoke drifted down from the Indian camp up the valley. The light dimmed so early this time of year, the shoulders of hills hulking in the gloom.

In the cabin, later, the squelch of juices and rasp of breathing under the heavy weight of wool blankets. Their skin sticking together like grasping hands. Her belly between them. Joseph's motions becoming frantic as he got closer, his arms shaking with the effort of keeping his weight up and off her. Her wanting him but concerned for the baby too.

Then, breaking in, the pig-like squeal of frantic horses. Joseph threw back the covers and stood, his member silhouetted against the red glow of the stove. He was a bear of a man—big and solid—yet he moved efficiently, smoothly, with economy of motion. He moved the way he was. The first time she had seen him in her father's tailor shop, she had thought he was dancing when all he was doing was moving crates.

Emmaline shivered as the cold air struck her sweaty skin, and she reached for the covers. Joseph grabbed his trousers from the floor and pulled them on, buttoning only one button, and then threw on his coat.

Crow? Emmaline said.

Joseph made a noncommittal sound as he pushed his feet into his boots and grabbed the Winchester. He slapped up the latch and pulled open the door and left it wide as he disappeared into the darkness. The crunch of his feet on the frozen grasses faded, and then there was nothing.

Emmaline lay with the covers up to her chin and listened. The frigid air streamed in the door and rapidly chilled the cabin's one room. The small cook stove was no match for it. Emmaline could feel the moistness of her breath against her cooling cheeks. She strained to hear a sound, anything. Was that hoof beats?

Reluctantly, she reached under the pillow and retrieved her nightgown. She sat up and quickly pulled it on, moving her head left to right to push through the neck hole. She threw back the covers and stood, remembering to flip them back over the bed so it would stay warm. She pushed the door almost closed and then put her ear to the crack. Still nothing. She shut the door, hooked the latch, and made sure the leather latch strings were threaded out through the holes so that Joseph could get back in. Then she went back to bed and listened.

After a long while, she heard the crunch of his boots and the slide of the latch as he let himself in.

Thank God, she said.

Probably a lion, he said. He opened the stove door and pushed in some wood splits. Next time, you throw something on and come.

She sat up in bed.

We got nothing if we in want of horses, he said. His hands were curled and black against the orange of the fire.

Billings, 1926

THE COURTROOM HAS A LINE OF SMALL WINDOWS high on the side wall. Through them, the morning light cuts a slanting swath to the floor, highlighting and truncating the curls of cigarette smoke. With the Thanksgiving chill in the air, the stove at the back of the room is lit, but it isn't the stove that causes the stifling heat—the courtroom is packed with people. It is a sensational, sensationalized case: two white men and an Indian rob a mercantile, and twenty-four hours later, one of the white men is dead.

From the front row of the jury box, Emmaline has a good view of the Indian boy when they bring him in. His skin is lighter than she expected. He is tall and slender, and his tight dark braid lays down his back in an upside-down question mark that cuts across the black and white prison stripes. He would be eighteen.

The boy looks over to the jury box for a long moment. He appraises each person without trying to hide it. His face does not change. When he looks at her, she looks away.

What must he see? An aging white woman. Emmaline knows she looks even older than she is, the way her flesh sags on her bones, the heavy streaks of gray in her hair, and her old-fashioned clothes that are a bit too formal for the modern woman. Maybe, too, it is her manner of shrinking away from the world, making herself smaller. Would he count her an ally or an enemy? She glances at the others in the jury box. There are no Indians. Of course there are no Indians. So she is just another one of the accusers, she supposes, an enemy.

During jury selection, it had been the prosecutor who had pushed to keep Emmaline. The defense attorney seemed indifferent. She wonders why. The prosecutor must've seen her as an ally. What about her made him think she was on his side? Or did he just think that she was easily persuaded?

The trial begins.

The prosecuting attorney, a tall thin man, clean-shaven, wearing a brown suit with a red bow tie, stands and gives his opening statement: Ladies and gentlemen of the jury, let me paint you a picture. It is a simple picture in black and white. Here it is: Two white men, down on their luck, find themselves in the hands of a renegade robber who plies them with bootleg liquor and persuades them to join him. This renegade plans to rob the Morrisey Mercantile at gun-point. These men are persuaded because—let's admit it—one, the departed Mr. Bonsieno, is simple, and the other, Mr. Charlie Greene, has a family, a wife and two young sons, back in Utah that he must provide for. The renegade robber, the same Mr. Jonah Sharp Beak who sits before you, he coerces the two men into helping him, and once he has the money he kills Mr. Bonsieno in cold blood, and Mr. Greene barely escapes with his life. Now, the defense will tell you there are what they'll call extenuating circumstances, but don't be fooled. This is a simple, if heinous, crime: Mr. Sharp Beak robbed the Morrisey Mercantile, killed Mr. Bonsieno, and will try to shift blame to Mr. Greene. Thank you.

The defense attorney, an older man with a face like a hound dog, stands and gives his opening statement: The prosecution would like you to believe that this is a simple case. That there is a villain—my client—and there are victims—not just the Morrisey Mercantile but also the other two men who perpetrated the robbery. But, ladies and gentlemen of the jury, as much as we would like to believe that the world is a simple place—that there are heroes and villains, winners and losers— that's just not true. I'm no Clarence Darrow, but even I know the world isn't black and white. Let's talk about black and white. What they didn't say—but what they want you to hear— is that this case is red and white. They want you to look at my client and see red and to look at the other two and see white. They want you to see my client, not as a fellow citizen of the United States, someone's beloved son struggling to make his way, but as an Indian. The term they use is renegade. They want you to think of him as the stereotype we read in dime- store novels. Ladies and gentlemen, as the prosecution said, don't be fooled. Yes, my client did participate in a robbery, but it was the two men, both almost twice my client's age and one a convicted felon, who persuaded an impressionable young man, against his better judgment, to join them, planning all the while to frame him for the crime. Please, vote on the side of justice, not of hatred.

As each man talks, Emmaline watches the boy. He sits very straight in his chair, as if he's in school. He looks straight ahead, and his face shows no expression, but Emmaline gets the feeling he's listening intently. He is like a deer who senses danger—still as a stone, alert to every sound and smell, yet ready to leap away at any second, only the manacles on his wrists and ankles discourage such ideas.

EMMALINE WAS IRONING HANDKERCHIEFS when Joseph brought the girl into the cabin by the arm. No matter what, Emmaline always ironed the handkerchiefs. It was her line in the sand, the level below which she would not sink. When Joseph caught her at it, he said nothing, only looked at her out of the corner of his eye. The small luxury of ironed handkerchiefs cost her time, time she should be baking next week's bread, churning the butter so that the cream didn't sour, and letting out a skirt so she would have something to wear in the coming months.

But when she did iron handkerchiefs, the iron's weight and heat through the wrapping cloth, the soothing steady motion, and the smell of steamy warm cotton made her so homesick for Iowa her stomach felt like a fist. All the family and friends she'd left behind. And with the coming child, she needed women friends in the worst way. She had only just reached out to the Calder woman five miles down the creek when winter shut down travel.

The baby kicked against the pressure of the table, and Emmaline smiled. She wanted this baby so much. Every time she thought about him—she just knew it was a boy—she felt buoyed upwards, lifted from the slog of the day. The feeling rose from her chest and pushed to her mouth and tried to crow from her lips.

The girl Joseph brought in had a blank look on her face like that of a pole-axed cow. She stood unmoving, wrapped in her woolen blanket in the corner next to the stove. The part in the girl's almost-black hair cleaved her round head in a perfect straight line and her oiled braids were so tight the dark brown skin was pulled taut. Her upper lip was wider than her lower lip, and her nose was round, almost like a negro's—not what Emmaline expected on a Crow. The girl was so thin her broad cheek bones stuck out over her jawbone.

Where's Bob? Emmaline said.

The gash was too deep, Joseph said. It 'as suppurated. Them up the creek might get a meal or two from him.

Emmaline stopped ironing and stood for a long moment, her head dropping to the side. Was there nothing to be done, then? she said.

Joseph looked at Emmaline and then looked away. You can ride the mare, he said. Come spring, we'll find a nice gelding. He walked over to her and laid his palm on her shoulder. It was warm and heavy and made Emmaline feel more solid. They were both so tired these days, they never seemed to touch during the day. Ten months married and already routine wore at them.

Emmaline looked over at the girl and then looked back over her shoulder to Joseph.

He shrugged. You in the way, he said, you'll soon need a body to help.

A child squaw? Emmaline lowered her voice. You, you bought her?

He shrugged again. She's called Fire something. You call her what you will. She'll work, they say. He turned and left the cabin.

Emmaline went to the door and watched him walk down the path to the creek carrying an axe. Then he stood where the path intersected the creek at a deep pool, and he bent his knees and then hefted and swung the axe into the ice. Chunk! He pulled it up and hefted it and swung again. Chunk! Emmaline could feel his body get into the rhythm of it—heft, swing, Chunk! pause, heft, swing, Chunk! pause. There was something about a job like chopping ice that soothed Joseph. He could see the results, and it was a physical task—he'd always been confident about his body. He'd won Emmaline's father's heart by mending the ailing sewing machine at the shop. He hadn't been nearly so comfortable with town society. Though he was a good dancer, he thought dances were pointless and would gather with the men who drank out back. He stayed for formal dinners just long enough to be polite. It was as if he were so bent on surviving, he forgot to live.

Emmaline had known this about him when she married him, but he made her feel safe. His physical confidence was hers. She felt like he could handle whatever came their way, and he could provide more than the bare living eked from a tailor shop. And it didn't hurt that when he came into the room she felt the urge to laugh so loudly at whatever conversation she was in so that he would hear and turn toward her, that the thought of him made her bubble inside.

Emmaline turned back to the girl. The girl's smell filled the cabin—thick wood smoke, rancid grease, sweat, and wet leather. It was a presence of its own. Emmaline held her breath until she had to let it out in a quick burst and then suck in through her mouth. She didn't want it to enter her, but she had little choice. The cabin was just one room. A bed next to the cast iron cook stove, a plank table and log bench, and two windows. Emmaline had fashioned curtains from cotton flour sacks, but the cheery yellow print disappeared in the gray winter light. After eight months, she had the cabin's contours memorized.

The girl would be hungry. Emmaline retrieved the leftover hasty pudding from the cabin's back window ledge. The girl moved aside as Emmaline opened the stove door, poked at the coals, and tossed in some kindling. She put a skillet on, scooped in some bacon grease to melt, and sliced the hasty pudding. Once the grease sputtered, Emmaline dropped the slices into the pan. The smell of bacon grease and frying corn meal filled the cabin.

The girl roused. She took a deep breath and watched Emmaline as Emmaline flipped the slices. Emmaline couldn't bring herself to smile, but she let her face relax and nodded slightly. The girl looked away. Emmaline put two slices on a tin plate to cool. She retrieved the pitcher of milk from the back window ledge and poured a mugful. She put the plate and the mug on the plank table. Almost as an afterthought, she laid a fork next to the plate. Then she turned to the girl.

You hungry? Emmaline said.

The girl's eyes were focused now on the food and she leaned forward onto her toes. Her chest rose and fell in quick succession. She didn't move, though. Emmaline walked over to her and reached to take her arm. The girl still didn't move, but something in her stance made Emmaline stop. There was a danger there—contained but just barely.

Well, it's for you when you want, Emmaline said. Maybe the girl didn't understand English. Emmaline turned and ignored her, putting more slices into the pan for her and Joseph's dinner. But Emmaline did watch the girl out of the corner of her eye. After a bit, the girl moved to the table and sat down. Emmaline expected her to attack the meal, maybe with her fingers, but instead the girl sat, bowed her head, and mumbled to herself.

Amen, the girl whispered.

Emmaline tried not to let the shock register on her face even though her back was turned.

The girl picked up the fork in her fist and cut a bit from the fried hasty pudding. Then she held it the correct way between her thumb and index finger and stabbed the piece and ate it. Her eyes closed as she swallowed. She continued eating, quickly cutting off pieces and forking them into her mouth. She ignored the milk. She was still eating quickly when she finished the last bit, so Emmaline put two more slices on her plate. The girl didn't look at her, just continued eating.

By the time Joseph returned, the girl had eaten three helpings. When the girl finished, she moved back to her post by the stove. There wasn't enough left for both Joseph and Emmaline, so Emmaline claimed that the sickness bothered her and ate bread and butter washed down by tea, though, with the child growing inside her, she was constantly hungry.

Emmaline watched Joseph eat while she sipped her tea.

She had sensed a wildness, a desperation, in Joseph at their first meeting. They were the same age—25, which made

Emmaline an old maid—but he had seemed much older, like his years had asked more of him. His letters had pleased her though. *The Nebraska prairie in the dying light looks so vast, I am humbled. It is only by thinking of you that I am comforted.* He seemed able to say things on paper he wouldn't—or couldn't—say in person. The words made her forget that warning voice, made her ache to have him near. When they met again, after having been apart for most of a year, she'd laughed at his beard and his shyness. *I'm going to have to civilize you again*, she'd said. He hadn't replied, just looked at her.

After supper, Emmaline made a pallet on the floor near the fire. It was all they had. There was no other bed. The girl accepted it with what seemed like gratitude—if not gratitude, at least without complaint. That night after they all went to bed, Emmaline's back ached, so she lay awake and listened to the breathing. Joseph's quickly transitioned from short worried breaths to long quiet even ones. At first she couldn't hear the girl's, but once Joseph's evened out, she could. She thought the girl was crying, but then she realized that the girl was asleep and it was a soft whine like a nervous dog.

Emmaline woke in the faint light of morning with the familiar menses spasms in her lower belly. But that couldn't be. She was pregnant. But it was true and they were worse than they'd ever been. Shortly after Joseph went to take care of the livestock, something broke and water gushed from inside her. The pain hit and seemed to take away the world. Someone was moaning and she realized it was her. Someone was laying a wet cloth on her forehead and it was the girl. The world was pain and everything else went away. At one point, there were arguing voices—her husband's loud but someone else's too, husky and soft, with a lilt, an accent, she'd never heard before.

The pain was there, and then it was less. And then she slept.

THE ROOM WHERE LUNCH IS SERVED TO THE JURORS smells of coal smoke, pipe tobacco, and oranges. The first day, Emmaline is the last to enter the room and, since there are not enough chairs around the central table, she takes the child's desk off to one side. As the trial continues, she finds she prefers this seat, as the other jurors argue incessantly over the details of the case even though the judge had told them not to discuss it outside deliberation hours. Emmaline refrains from asserting her opinion. It isn't in her nature to assert.

Besides, she feels coerced every time one of the shouters looks her direction for support, and Emmaline hates feeling coerced. She hasn't lived forty-three years and survived countless disasters and an angry husband to be shouted at.

There's no denying it—her husband had been an angry man. It was an anger that stemmed from Joseph's striving, from the way the world seemed to deny him. In fact, it seemed in the end it was the anger that ate him from the inside out, although the diagnosis had been cancer of the pancreas. Sure, there were years in the middle of their marriage where she found ways to ameliorate it, to diffuse the meaninglessness and meanness of it. If asked, she might've even said she was happy. But it was a thread that pulled tight and wrinkled the cloth of their lives.

If only there had been a child, she thinks, maybe things would have been different.

SPRING BROKE THE BACK OF WINTER. The snowdrifts under the north eaves contracted until they were nothing more than a muddy patch dotted with green shoots. There were wet smells—the smell of rain, the smell of mud, the smell of things growing. The new leaves were always rustling in the breeze. The first greens of the year tasted so sweet they might have been touched with honey. The frigid fingers of wind grew softer, warmer.

Joseph seemed around less with the girl there. Emmaline wasn't sure if it was that he avoided the cabin or that she just noticed his absences less. He had plenty to do that kept him away. Spring brought clearing ditches, planting, tending birthing cattle and sheep, and helping their few neighbors. When he sat in his chair in the evening, his jaw worked as he stared into the fire. Emmaline felt the urge to pet his hair to try to sooth that troubled jaw. Even in the night, he rarely turned to her. It was as if her belly, empty though it was, still came between them. It was as if his want of her had diminished. She wondered if it was because she had failed, or was it because the girl slept only a few feet away.

Emmaline named the girl Ruth, which the girl answered to without comment. Ruth could speak lilting English but rarely did so. After her initial tentativeness, she settled in and seemed happy at her work, willing—cheerful, even, in her quiet way.

One day during breakfast, Joseph watched Ruth. Ruth, for her part, didn't seem to notice. She ate her usual second helping before clearing the dishes and taking them to the porch to wash. Rather than rising immediately to attend to his work, Joseph sat for a minute.

What's wrong? Emmaline said.

Joseph did not hesitate. The girl eats like a striking miner, he said. She's getting fat.

Ruth works hard.

Maybe, but she eats too much.

Emmaline had noticed Ruth's hearty appetite too but she did not begrudge it. Ruth had been so skinny when she joined them, Emmaline imagined her trying to catch up for years of starvation. Plus Emmaline's world had been rocked like a San Francisco earthquake, which left her ice-numb and empty. Her appetite had all but gone away. The less she was reminded of her body, the better. She had been so full before—full of baby, full of hunger, full of promise—but now there was nothing inside her. It was the inverse of wanting. The hollowness consumed her. That's why Ruth's appetite felt good, felt right—when she watched Ruth eat she felt just a little more full.

Do you want me to deny her? Emmaline said.

Joseph said nothing as he stood and put on his jacket.

Are you saying you want me to withhold food?

I'll leave you to it, he said and left.

At first, Joseph had been kind to Ruth. He had asked if she was comfortable, if she had everything she needed. Ruth wouldn't answer, but her shoulders would relax just a bit. He even tried to coax a laugh from her, but the most he got was a glance out of the corner of Ruth's eye. Emmaline had been so grateful for this because she wanted Ruth to have kindness. The way Ruth's body would freeze in thought made Emmaline wonder about her life before. But then Joseph got quiet. He never leaned back against the table and propped on his elbows anymore—he always sat curled forward like a fist. He would look from Emmaline to Ruth and back again. Before Ruth, they had barely touched during the day, but now when Ruth was around, Joseph put his arm around Emmaline and pull her to him and ignore the rules of simple propriety.

Emmaline stood in the middle of the kitchen. There next to the stove was Ruth's bed. Next to it, a low log stuck out to form a natural shelf, and on it rested a bird's feather, a scrap of leather, and a bone hair clip Emmaline had given her. A sound welled up inside Emmaline and sought to escape her windpipe, but she held it down.

Ruth returned with the dried dishes and put them away.

What was it like before, Emmaline said, before you came to us?

Ruth stopped and turned and raised her eyebrows.

Did your people treat you well? Emmaline said.

After a minute, Ruth said, They weren't my people.

You're not Crow?

Ruth flinched at her question. After a long minute she spoke: It is the custom where I came from—where I came from before—to name a child after an important event. An elder gives the name. It was a cold winter, the winter I was born. Crazy Sister in Law hunted in the hills when a snow storm hit. He could not make his way back to the tents. He was near freezing in the lee of the pines when through the white came a man. He was of a tribe never seen before. He wasn't of the black tribe that joined our tribe or of your white tribe from the East. He had bright eyes and a sharp nose and a red breast plate. Crazy Sister in Law knew then that he was of the Robin Clan. He brought fire so that Crazy Sister in Law could live.

Ruth looked Emmaline in the eyes. Ruth said, That's why I was named Fire Giver.

Someone had cared enough to give Ruth this name. It was as if a room had opened up behind Ruth. Emmaline could see its hearth and the pallets for beds and the paintings on the walls. It was warm and there were people, kind loving people talking and working and laughing. So different from what she had imagined before—the starvation, the beatings, worse. Maybe there had been that too, later, but at least there was this.

Ruth said, We bake today, *Nawkohe*?

It was a warm day, a good day for the bread to rise. Emmaline mixed the sourdough starter into the flour and added a touch of honey and salt. Then she gave the bowl to Ruth for Ruth to knead and turned to begin the noon meal.

Ruth hummed as she worked the dough. With the labor and the heat of the day, she shed her outer shirt so that Emmaline could see her shoulders as their muscles bunched and relaxed. There was something awkward about the way Ruth moved. She bent over farther than necessary. At first, Emmaline thought maybe her back bothered her, but the humming belied it. It was as if she were avoided the table edge with the front of her hips. Emmaline walked around to the side. There it was—the belly rounded, extended. Ruth was in the way.

Frantically, Emmaline counted the months. Could it be? The strange way Joseph had been acting. Could it be, rather than a simple horse trade, that it was Joseph's child? No. It couldn't be. Ruth was at least six months gone, and she had only been with them three. Then Emmaline blushed at her own impertinence. It had to have been before. It was not Joseph's child.

Still, she felt betrayed. She grabbed Ruth's arm, which flipped sideways and flour clouded the air. Startled, arm in the air, Ruth looked at Emmaline's face and then followed her eyes down to her own belly.

Like you, Ruth said.

It was like Emmaline. All women were equal under the weight of childbearing. It happened without their say and yet each in their turn could die from it. The anger drained from her. She wanted to ask, why? You're only a child. She wanted to ask who the father was. She wanted to ask whether it was someone who the girl had loved.

But she couldn't. Of course she couldn't. Instead she put her hands on Ruth's belly and felt its solidity. Ruth squared her shoulders, offering her belly to Emmaline. Then she extended her hands around Emmaline's arms and pressed them to the front of Emmaline's dress, to her flat belly. Flour fell and streaked the front of Emmaline's skirt.

Then a laugh bubbled up inside Emmaline. It churned and gurgled and made its way out of her throat and escaped her mouth. It tickled her nose. Ruth looked at her strangely and then laughed too. The two women stood, holding each other's bellies, and laughed.

THE TRIAL DRAGS ON. As much as Emmaline tries, she can't concentrate. The heat and the smell of bodies and the wreak of smoke bring on the headaches.

She has been plagued with headaches, especially in her middle years. They start at the top of her spine and pound their way up and over the top of her head till they shut down her eyes. She knows that when she sees the telltale glow around everything that she'd better lie down, but she always puts it off for as long as possible, hoping this time it will go away of its own accord.

That was why, when Joseph began to hold his side as he sat at the dinner table, to make a sound at the back of his throat like he was trying to clear an obstruction, Emmaline begged him to lie down, to take it easy. But he wouldn't, of course— not that she expected him to. For a while, his anger focused on her, as if the pain in his abdomen was her fault, but near the end he changed.

It was a few days before the end that he looked at her and said, I don't want to die. He was lying in his bed, his bones rounded protrusions under his skin, which, along with his eyes, were the yellow of unripe tomatoes. He seemed a child rolled in poison ivy, the way he fidgeted and itched incessantly.

His eyes sought her face. He focused and said it louder, this time an upturn in his voice: I don't want to die.

Emmaline said nothing. There was nothing to say. She just brought the bowl of broth closer to his chin and dipped the spoon.

In a feeble gesture, he batted the bowl away, which fell to the floor and spattered broth in an oval splash pattern away from the bed. Emmaline jumped to the side to avoid the hot liquid. The bowl did not break, though. It curled around and around on its lip, making a continuous sound until quicker and quicker it circled to a stop with a plop.

I'm sorry, Emmaline, he said. I know I come up wanting. All I ever tried to do was make a life for us, for you. You know that, don't you?

Emmaline thought she did know that. It was just the animal anger that had kept him silent and fierce. It was an animal Emmaline could not approach.

Emmaline pulls herself back to the trial. When lunch break is called, she closes her eyes, puts her head down on the desk, and tries to empty her mind.

AUGUST BROUGHT A BLANKET OF HEAT THAT SUFFOCATED EVEN THE PLANTS. The distant hills looked wavy as if viewed through the ripples in a pool, and the buzzing of the cicadas overwhelmed all other sound. The cows lolled in the shade along the creek and wore deep muddy grooves under the willows. Emmaline tried to serve cold dishes, and when she had to cook, she tried to get it out of the way in the cool of the morning. Her garden wilted in the heat of the day and she worried that some of the weaker plants might die—they could ill-afford the loss. They slept with the door and both windows open and prayed for a breeze.

Emmaline and Joseph still slept in the same bed, but Emmaline hugged the wall and Joseph teetered on the edge. It had begun the day Emmaline found out Ruth was pregnant. At dinner, she had served Ruth herself and had heaped the plate full. Ruth had glanced at her but said nothing. Joseph's eyes widened and his jaw worked, but he said nothing either. This began the weeks of saying nothing. They got by on the bare minimum of communication. What Emmaline couldn't ask for herself, she demanded for Ruth without saying a word. She laid the extra blanket on Ruth's pallet. She noticed that Ruth loved canned peaches, so she wrote them on the list when Joseph made his monthly trek to town for supplies. If Joseph even looked Ruth's way, Emmaline was there, standing between them, looking right back at him.

Ruth had indeed grown fat, not just large with child. She was round from her head to her toes—from her once-sunken cheeks to her soft shoulders to her squared hips to her solid ankles. Even her moods were rounded smiles and bubbly chuckles under her breath. It felt good just to be in the same room with her.

The time came for Ruth's baby. Emmaline gave her the easiest tasks but Ruth grew restless. Ruth was soaking her swollen feet in a cool basin of water and tipping green beans and snapping them into thirds. She stopped and made a low sound. Her eyes were dark and wide.

Emmaline nodded. She stripped the bed and laid extra linen on it. She helped Ruth down to her long white undershirt and laid her in the bed. She ladled a basin full of water cool from the creek and brought it to the bedside with a cloth. She wet the cloth and gave it to Ruth to dab her chest and forehead. She pulled a log stool next to the bed. She gathered an old copy of *Ladies Home Journal* and the Bible and sat. She used the magazine to fan Ruth and opened the Bible and read from the book of Jonah. As Emmaline read, Ruth's pains came and went, but other than a wrinkle in her brow, Emmaline could not tell.

Emmaline read: The sea wrought and was tempestuous. And Jonah said unto the sailors, take me up, and cast me forth into the sea, so shall the sea be calm unto you for I know that for my sake this great tempest is upon you. So they took Jonah up and cast him forth into the sea, and the sea ceased raging. Now the Lord had prepared a great fish to swallow up Jonah.

And Jonah was in the belly of the fish three days and three nights. Then Jonah prayed unto the Lord his God out of the fish's belly: The waters compassed me about, even to the soul. The depth closed me round about. The weeds were wrapped about my head. And the Lord spake unto the fish, and it vomited out Jonah upon the dry land.

Like me, Ruth said, her hands rubbing her belly.

Emmaline stopped reading.

They cast me into the sea and then others took me up and spat me out.

Who? Emmaline said.

Do you think a one God would do that?

He brought you to me in my time of need.

This made Ruth smile.

Ruth labored through the day and into the night. Joseph grumbled as he rustled up his own dinner of bread in milk and made a pallet on the porch to sleep the night. In the dark hours of the morning, a fat boy baby was born. Ruth named him Jonah. Out of the whale's belly, she said and laughed.

After Ruth put Jonah to her breast, Emmaline washed him while Ruth slept. Emmaline laid linen and a basin of warm water on the table and laid Jonah on it. She unwrapped him from the blanket and dipped a cloth in water and began to gently scrub. He had a fuzz of dark hair haloing his head and ears like tiny shelf mushrooms. His eyes seemed too large for his face as he stared up at her. His mouth was tiny and the lips moved and the tongue stuck out like he was trying to figure out how it all worked. His chubby little arms and legs curled against his round belly. Even his toes were perfect little peas. As Emmaline washed, his bark-colored skin reddened. His eyes remained wide as if he were trying to take it all in. Once he was washed, Emmaline wrapped him back in his blanket and held him to her chest and rocked him, humming the same tune over and over, an old tune that had no name.

A week passed. Then another. Emmaline and Ruth developed a rhythm of taking care of Jonah. Emmaline ignored Joseph's dour looks.

Joseph rode to town for supplies. When he returned the next day, he led a large bay horse with their supplies in its panniers. He unloaded the panniers and then let both horses out to pasture. A man rode up as he finished. He and the man talked for a while before coming in to lunch.

When she saw them talking, Emmaline hastily made biscuits and opened a can of pickles. The stew would run short. She had Ruth set an extra place.

This is Dick Linstrom, Joseph said as he led the man into the house. Runs the general store there in Pahaska.

The man was short and thin with wide-open eyes than made him look like an innocent. He removed his hat as Joseph spoke.

Pleased to meet you, Emmaline said.

The man nodded in Emmaline's direction but his eyes were on Ruth. Emmaline had an urge to step between them then.

And this is Ruth, Joseph said.

Emmaline looked at Joseph. She had expected him to ignore Ruth. His head stuck forward on his shoulders and his teeth clenched just a bit like he was expecting a blow. Then Emmaline looked back at Ruth in a panic.

Ruth looked from Joseph to the man and then moved over to her pallet and picked up Jonah.

And this is her baby, Joseph said.

The man furrowed his brow and looked over at Joseph. The man said, You never said…

Joseph shrugged.

Emmaline felt panic rise in her then. Joseph had done something. What was it? What had he done? Still she said, Would you like to sit down to dinner?

Joseph sat at his place at the head of the table, Emmaline sat at the foot, Ruth sat next to the wall holding Jonah, and the man sat opposite. They said grace and served, and the man immediately complimented Emmaline on the meal. Mighty fine biscuits, ma'am, he said. Then he turned to Ruth. How old's your baby?

Ruth, who had been focusing on her plate and Jonah, didn't seem to hear his question.

Ruth, Joseph said, Mr. Linstrom asked you a question.

Emmaline gave Joseph a look down the table, but Joseph refused to look at her.

Sorry? Ruth said.

Your baby, the man said, how old is it?

He's just been born, Ruth said. Two weeks tomorrow.

Does taking care of a baby take a lot out of you? the man said. The question seemed to be aimed at both Ruth and Emmaline.

When Ruth didn't say anything, Emmaline said, She does all right. Panic welled up inside her. What could she say that would stop this? Whatever it was.

She does all right, Joseph said, nodding. Plus, women love babies. Couldn't hurt business. When Joseph said this, he shrugged.

All right, then, the man said as he scooped stew into his mouth.

Joseph, Emmaline said, what's, um, how was your trip to Pahaska? Did you, say, buy a horse? As she said this, she tried to pin his eyes with hers.

A fine horse, Mrs. Connor, the man said. He's eighteen hands, a real worker, and might I say it was awful generous of you to let go your help here.

Emmaline looked at the man for a minute trying to register what he said.

Yes ma'am, the man said, Joseph was telling me about what a good worker she is. And here I am needing a woman— at this he glanced over at Ruth—ahem, a female person to make the store all friendly and help out, you see. The man bowed his head and said, Sorry to hear 'bout you losing your stud and all.

Then Emmaline knew. Just as Joseph had bought Ruth, now he sold her. Oh, he may not have couched it in those terms. Maybe he kicked in some money and told the man he needed just a little incentive to let Ruth go. Maybe the stud represented Ruth's first year's salary.

Joseph, Emmaline said, can I talk with you for a moment on the porch?

Emmaline, we'll talk after Mr. Linstrom has gone. When he said it, he threw his gaze down the length of the table like he'd swung an axe. It hit home in her eyes and stayed there. His face was utterly still for a moment. Emmaline glanced away and down and her glance caught his hands. They were to the left of his plate fiddling with a knife. It was his skinning knife, the one he used at the table to cut gristled meat. This was neither an idle nor a pointed touch—rather, as if he was feeling its contours, cogitating.

Emmaline took an involuntary breath. Her head filled with possibilities she had never imagined before. She felt her hands begin to shake as adrenalin shot threw her body. She looked over at Ruth. Ruth's deep eyes were on her face. What Ruth saw Emmaline would never know, but then Ruth looked over at the man and said, I get paid plus a living?

The man nodded.

Emmaline was forming her lips into syllables, even with those hands fiddling down the table, when Ruth put her hand on Emmaline's.

You married? Ruth said to the man.

The man looked startled at the question. His head pulled backwards and then he shook it back and forth in a small motion.

Well, I'm not looking to get married, Ruth said. Then Ruth looked down the table toward Joseph. Emmaline couldn't see Ruth's face, but she saw Joseph's. At first he met her eyes but the silence drew on and on and then he pulled back a little and finally he let his gaze drop to his hands, which now lay wilted and open.

Ruth turned back to Emmaline. She smiled at Emmaline and shrugged. Sometimes there are whales, she said.

Supper done, it only took a minute for Ruth to roll her few things into her blanket and to swaddle Jonah tightly to her body. When the man mounted his horse, Joseph swung Ruth up behind the man. Emmaline watched from the porch. The last she saw of Ruth was her outline fading into the form of the man. Ruth did not look back.

IT IS AS IF THE DELIBERATING ROOM HAS BECOME EMMALINE'S HOME. They've been in it for three days, with no signs of leaving, and it has undergone that change that occurs between when a person first enters a place and when they've lived in it for a while. It becomes unconscious, a part of them. Emmaline does not want this building to be a part of her.

With what do you support your position? the foreman, one of the shouters, says.

Emmaline shakes her head. She says, How can you say you believe he did it when it's his word against a convict's?

Another juror, the only other woman, says, You don't believe that malarkey about him being so young, do you? It doesn't matter, with them. Isn't that right, Jack? She looks over to the foreman for support.

The foreman says, Now, Mrs. Frabricci, we must not let emotions get the better of us. Then he turns to Emmaline. Is that it? Is it his age?

Emmaline shakes her head. She says, That's not it. What it comes down to is that the boy is innocent unless they can show otherwise, and the only evidence they have is the word of an old convict who can't keep his story straight anyhow.

Another man, who'd sat forward and watched the trial as if it were a tennis match, says, Be reasonable. This is our third day. We all believe he's guilty, all except you. What do you want? Do you think you're so much smarter than us? Even if you do, don't you want to get this over with?

She did want this over with. But simply having it over wasn't enough. During the first day of deliberations, when the two others who had been voting to acquit decided to vote for guilt, something within her had solidified. It wasn't just that the ones for guilt were so loud and so convinced of their position. It was as if a part of her remembered a time when she held opinions of her own, a time when she had been given fire. What could happen if she held to what she truly felt in her heart? Did it matter? They could do nothing to her, and it wasn't herself she was doing it for. That made it easier.

All right, the foreman says. Let's take a poll. This is our last—make the most of it. He looks at Emmaline as he says this. They vote and it comes up as it has for the last day and a half: eleven votes guilty, one vote not guilty. They are a hung jury, and there is nothing else to be done.

Why? the other woman hisses as they enter the courtroom. It's not because of the convict.

Emmaline just shakes her head. How can she tell them that when she looks at the boy, she remembers the face of a fat brown girl with severe braids. That, in the Jonah's length and breadth, she sees toes like baby peas and ears like tiny shelf mushrooms and a tongue just trying to figure itself out.

Acknowledgements

These stories would not be possible without the help of so many people.

To Rachel Stout and to everyone at Dystel & Goderich Literary Management, thank you for believing in my work.

If these stories have any merit, thank my many teachers: Alyson Hagy, Vicki Lindner, John D'Agata, Tom McGuane, Whitney Otto, Dennis Lehane, Les Standiford, Michael Czyzniejewski, Jill Meyers, Steve Almond, Katherine Noel, Chitra Divakaruni, Jim Shepard, Luis Alberto Urrea, Caitlin Horrocks, Shann Ray, and Danielle Evans. The faults are all my own, however. I would also like to thank my many professors in the University of Wyoming English Department.

My writing friends have kept me going when all else failed: Nina, Jessica, Kerry, Meg, April, Patty, Pierre, Rashena, Ken, and Rachel. And there are so many more of you—I've missed many names, and for that I'm sorry. I'd also like to thank my Project 365 friends, whose creativity inspires my own.

To the many wonderful literary magazines that I've read and loved and who have published me—yours is a labor of love, and we writers love you!

All the people I worked with at TRC Mariah Associates Inc. and at the University of Wyoming Foundation have been so encouraging—thank you!

Families make all manner of things possible, and I would like to thank the Tilletts and the Linses—especially Marian Tillett who read me Shakespeare as a child and Jean Linse who is my Ideal Reader—as well as my honorary family members (you know who you are). These stories owe a lot to you all.

213

Acknowledgements

Last and certainly not least I would like to thank Steve, Eli, and Elizabeth, whom I love with all my heart.

– Tamara Linse, Laramie, Wyoming, 2013

Find Tamara Linse on the web:

www.tamaralinse.com
tamara-linse.blogspot.com
@tamaralinse
fb.com/tlinse

Reading Group Guide

How to Be a Man
Tamara Linse

"Never acknowledge the fact that you're a girl, and take pride when your guy friends say, 'You're one of the guys.' Tell yourself, 'I am one of the guys,' even though, in the back of your mind, a little voice says, 'But you've got girl parts.'" – Birdie, in "How to Be a Man"

A girl whose self-worth revolves around masculinity, a bartender who loses her sense of safety, a woman who compares men to plants, and a boy who shoots his cranked-out father. These are a few of the hard-scrabble characters in Tamara Linse's debut short story collection, *How to Be a Man*. Set in contemporary Wyoming—the myth of the West taking its toll—these stories reveal the lives of tough-minded girls and boys, self-reliant women and men, struggling to break out of their lonely lives and the emotional havoc of their families to make a connection, to build a life despite the odds. *How to Be a Man* falls within the traditions of Maile Meloy, Tom McGuane, and Annie Proulx.

The author Tamara Linse—writer, cogitator, recovering ranch girl—broke her collarbone when she was three, her leg when she was four, a horse when she was twelve, and her heart ever since. Raised on a ranch in northern Wyoming, she earned her master's in English from the University of Wyoming, where she taught writing. Her work appears in the *Georgetown Review*, *South Dakota Review*, and *Talking River*, among others, and she was a finalist for an Arts & Letters and *Glimmer Train* contests, as well as the Black Lawrence Press Hudson Prize for a book of short stories. She works as an editor for a foundation and a freelancer. Find her online at tamaralinse.com and tamara-linse.blogspot.com.

Letter from the Author

The stories in *How to Be a Man* were written over the course of the last fifteen years. Some came hot and fast and did not need much fiddling ("Men Are Like Plants," "Oranges") and some were the result of years of revision ("Nose to the Fence," "Mouse"). The oldest story in the collection is "Snowshoeing," and it's flaws make me uncomfortable, but I love the striving to capture something inexplicable that motivated it. The youngest story is "Dammed," and it's a good example of my writing process now—I tend to revise extensively as I go and write a lot in my mind before I put it down on the page. Once I get started, it only takes me a session or two to get it all down.

Author's often get the question, "Where do you get your ideas?" I've never had a problem getting ideas, and I mourn the loss of the multitude of ideas that have come and gone, unfulfilled. I think there are lots of ideas out there—it's just a matter of recognizing them for what they are, and when I'm writing—not blocked—the ideas come thick and fast. I may start with a voice, which happened with "Men Are Like Plants." I was lying in bed trying to go to sleep, and her voice came to me so strongly I risked my husband's displeasure—he hates it when I stay up late—and got up to write it down. I wrote most of that story in one sitting. What prompted "Revelations" was a contest a couple of years ago that had to include the year 2010. It got me thinking about the end of the world and Revelations, and so I wondered what a modern-day devil might be like. "Snowshoeing" started with the idea of conveying that feeling of separateness that sometimes comes upon a couple, that realization that you can't always take your partner for granted. "Oranges" arose in one sitting on a plane coming back from a writer's conference, the result of guilt over abandoning my kids for a week. "A Dangerous Shine" is based on a real incident that took place at the Buckhorn where I bartended. And on it goes.

Putting together a collection is tough. The idea of revising so many stories at one time and the nakedness that will result from other people seeing them all together is enough to stop the hardiest souls in their tracks. And what order do you put them in? Do you treat them like a mix tape—starting with an attention grabber, turning it up, taking it back, orchestrating peaks and valleys? Or do you arrange them on merit only, putting the best ones first? My protagonists are of different ages—should they be organized by age? I ended up putting what I think of as my best stories first and last, but then also taking into account the mood of the story. I tried to start with some positive stories and then place some of the darkest stories toward the end. I also tried to group them tonally, thematically, and by protagonist, so "Mouse" and "Oranges" are together because they're about young girls dealing with their parents. "The Body Animal," "Revelations," and "Dammed" are together because they're about the body and violence and alienation. "Wanting" is last because it's a strong story but it also is historical, while all the others are contemporary.

I've always loved when authors tell the story of the story, and so I thought I'd choose a few and talk about how they came into being. "How to Be a Man" was written in response to "How to Date a Browngirl, Blackgirl, Whitegirl, or Halfie" by Junot Diaz. I had long resisted writing a second-person story because it seemed so cliché—the young writer thinking herself so edgy, taking such an avant garde point of view. Then I read a couple of kick-ass second-person stories, and it began to work on me: Why couldn't I write one? Then I heard Edwidge Danticat read Diaz's story and I was hooked. The story wrote itself fairly quickly until I got to the ending—well, the first ending where she becomes a whiskery-chinned old batty. I stopped there. But I didn't like that ending. I didn't want her life to end that way. I wanted her to have a chance at happiness. Then I thought, why can't I have two endings. I'm the god in this little world. I can do whatever I want. So I added the second ending. "Wanting" is another story I wrote in response to a story. Growing up in the West, I had strong Hemingway tendencies—clipped sentences, withheld emotion, huge psychic distance—and so to try to remedy that, I decided to take a great story that was a little more lush to imitate it in sentence construction, paragraphing, even down to where the dialog rests. The story I chose was Karl Iagnemma's "Children of Hunger." So I tried to maintain the feel of his story and mimicked it as closely as I could in my own story. It was a very helpful exercise, I think, and I really like the results. "Mouse" began as a writer's exercise at a conference workshop presided over by Steve Almond. He had good advice about the mouse-killing scene: "A little blood and gore goes a long way." I later expanded the scene into the story.

I will always write short stories. They are harder than novels, in a way, because they require the precision of a diamond cutter. They have to be so much more concise, clear, compact, and well-written than a novel. In a novel, you can get away with pages of loose extraneous stuff, while a short story must have no fat. And I love reading short stories. I think we're in a renaissance of good short-story writing, and for that I'm very thankful.

Happy reading!

— Tamara Linse, Laramie, Wyoming, 2013

Discussion Questions

1. In "Control Erosion" and "Men Are Like Plants," the protagonists' takes on the world are deeply affected by their jobs. How are Linse's characters defined by their work, on and off the job? Is there something about living in the American West that makes one's job more, or less, important? How does class interact with occupation in these stories? How does Linse's portrayal of people in the West differ from ones you've read before?

2. Families are often struggling or even broken in Linse's fiction. The mother in "Oranges" is doing her best but is drowning in alcohol. The father in "Mouse" is nurturing, but his pragmatism often supersedes that. What social forces are at work behind these strained relationships? Is there something specific about the American West that

causes strains within families? What do you think will happen to these families after these stories end?

3. The characters in "Revelations" and "Snowshoeing" do some pretty horrible things. Which characters did you identify with? Which did you revile? Is it important to "like" the characters? Is it important that they get their just desserts in the end?

4. The end of "Nose to the Fence" is positive, while the end to "The Body Animal" is without hope. The ending of "In the Headlights" is ambiguous. Are happy endings important to you? Do you like tidy endings, even if they are tragedies? Do you like "epiphanic" endings, where the protagonist realizes something? Or do you like ambiguous endings that provide closure without resolution?

5. The romantic relationships in many of these stories have small moments of connection, while overall the characters struggle with loneliness. Are you rooting for these relationships? Or would you like a more traditional romantic arc? Do some of these relationships seem beyond hope?

6. Violence is a thread snagging underneath the cloth of these stories. In "Hard Men," a boy becomes a killer and a felon. In "Revelations," characters not only attack each other, but they also are emotionally violent to each other. The dad in "Mouse" is loving but hard. Do you think the West has a particular tendency toward violence? Or is it peculiarly American? What would be a solution to the problem of violence in these families?

7. The American West is a particularly masculine culture, and the girls and women in these stories struggle to reconcile what they are with their own self-worth and agency. Is this the case in other cultures around the world? What traits do these societies have in common? How do women cope with this in these stories?

8. Do you like the title, "How to Be a Man"? Do you think it's misleading? How does it fit? What does the cover convey about the collection's contents? If you were going to design a cover for the collection, what images would you include? What genres do these stories fit into?

9. The history of the American West and the genre of the Western rests heavily in the background of these stories. Where do you see the genre of the Western show through? What would a contemporary Western look like? How do women fit in the modern Western? What other authors have you read that explore the modern West?

10. What themes do the stories have in common? Do they differ according to whether the protagonist is female or male? Which parts of our society are not represented in these stories? Do you think that's a failure of imagination on the author's part or a reflection of contemporary Wyoming?

11. Linse's characters, while resourceful and creative, often live anachronistic lives disconnected from technology and other advantages that many of us take for granted. Is there evidence in these stories that the characters are capable of coping with the

challenges and demands of daily life, work, and love in the twenty-first century?

12. These stories take place in rural communities and small towns. How might the plots of the stories and the lives of the characters change if played in urban settings?

About the Author

Tamara Linse grew up on a ranch in northern Wyoming with her farmer/rancher rock-hound ex-GI father, her artistic musician mother from small-town middle America, and her four sisters and two brothers. She jokes that she was raised in the 1880s because they did things old-style—she learned how to bake bread, break horses, irrigate, change tires, and be alone, skills she's been thankful for ever since. The ranch was a partnership between her father and her uncle, and in the 80s and 90s the two families had a Hatfields and McCoys-style feud.

She worked her way through the University of Wyoming as a bartender, waitress, and editor. At UW, she was officially in almost every college on campus until she settled on English and after 15 years earned her bachelor's and master's in English. While there, she taught writing, including a course called Literature and the Land, where students read Wordsworth and Donner Party diaries during the week and hiked in the mountains on weekends. She also worked as a technical editor for an environmental consulting firm.

She still lives in Laramie, Wyoming, with her husband Steve and their twin son and daughter. She writes fiction around her job as an editor for a foundation. She is also a photographer, and when she can she posts a photo a day for a Project 365. Please stop by Tamara's website, *www.tamaralinse.com*, and her blog, Writer, Cogitator, Recovering Ranch Girl, at *tamara-linse.blogspot.com*. You can find an extended bio there with lots of juicy details. Also friend her on Facebook and follow her on Twitter, and if you see her in person, please say hi.

Made in the USA
San Bernardino, CA
11 April 2015